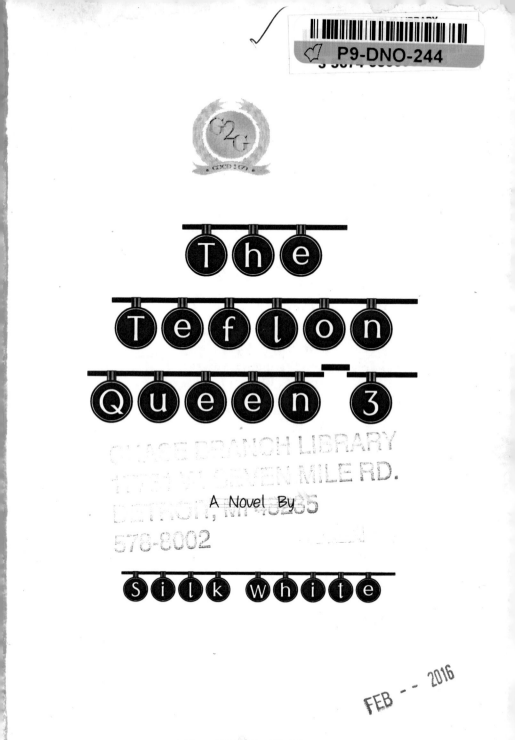

The Teflon Queen 3

A Novel By

Silk White

Good2Go Publishing

Good2Go Publishing

This novel is a work of fiction. All the characters, organizations, establishments, and events portrayed in this novel are either product of the author's imagination or are fiction.

GOOD2GO PUBLISHING
7311 W. Glass Lane
Laveen, AZ 85339
Copyright © 2014 by Silk White
www.good2gopublishing.com
twitter @good2gobooks
G2G@good2gopublishing.com
Facebook.com/good2gopublishing
ThirdLane Marketing: Brian James
Brian@good2gopublishing.com
Cover design: Davida Baldwin
Editor: Kesha Buckhana
Typesetter: Harriet Wilson
ISBN: 9780989185981
Printed in the United States of America
10 9 6 7 6 5 4 3 2 1

Books By This Author

Married To Da Streets
Never Be The Same
Stranded
Tears of a Hustler
Tears of a Hustler 2
Tears of a Hustler 3
Tears of a Hustler 4
Tears of a Hustler 5
Teflon Queen
Teflon Queen 2
Teflon Queen 3

Acknowledgments

To you reading this right now. Thank you for stepping inside the bookstore, stopping by the library, or downloading a copy of The Teflon Queen 3. I hope you have enjoyed this read from top to bottom. My goal is to get better and better with each story. I want to thank everyone for all their love and support. It is definitely appreciated!
Now without further ado Ladies and Gentleman, I give you **"The Teflon Queen 3"**. ENJOY!!!

$iLK WHiTE

Intro

"Come on we have to go...," Randy said looking over both shoulders in the mall as he held a firm grip on his daughter's hand and pulled her along.

"But daddy I'm tired," Ashley whined. Her little twelve-year-old legs were tired and needed a rest. She didn't quite understand why they had to move so quickly.

Randy glanced over his shoulder one last time before slipping off into the men's room. Once inside the bathroom Randy grabbed the garbage can and slid it in front of the door.

"Daddy I'm tired. Can we..."

"Shut up!" Randy snapped as he shoved his hand down in his pocket and removed a thumb drive. "Ashley listen to me carefully," he said squatting down so he could look his daughter in the eye. "No matter what happens, you keep this with you at all times. I don't care what happens. Do you understand?"

Ashley nodded her head up and down.

"What did I just say?" Randy quizzed her.

"No matter what happens to keep this with me at all times," Ashley repeated with a scared look on her face.

"And don't show it to no one! You hear, and I mean no one!" he stressed as he slipped the thumb drive down into Ashley's front pocket. "I love you," Randy said as he hugged his daughter tightly. Seconds later the bathroom door came crashing open and in stepped five hard faced men.

"Randy! Randy! Randy!" the leader of the pack spoke. He was a Caucasian man with a rugged beard. "You really disappointed me and you really disappointed Mr. Clarke."

"What do you want from me?" Randy asked.

"Don't play stupid with me. You know what the fuck I want!" the leader barked. "Hand it over and everyone can walk away from here alive," he lied.

"I don't know what you're talking about," Randy said with a straight face. Without warning, the leader of the pack removed a .45 from his shoulder holster and slapped Randy across the face with it, sending blood splattering all over the bathroom mirror. He then grabbed Randy by the collar of his shirt and pressed the barrel of the gun an inch deep into his temple.

"Last time I'm going to ask you! Where... is... it?" the leader asked through clenched teeth.

"Hold on! You ain't gon get it if you kill me," Randy protested. "Let me speak to Mr. Clarke and see if we can work something out."

"Mr. Clarke is done talking. He already made you an offer. You declined and now here I am," the leader told him. "Now you got to the count of three to give me what I came here for or else I'm going to splatter your brains all over this bathroom," he threatened.

"Come on this really isn't necessary," Randy, pleaded.

"One," the leader began counting off.

"Please don't do this; please," Randy begged.

"Two..."

Having no other options, Randy grabbed the leader's wrist and tried to wrestle the gun out of his hands. "Ashley run!!!" he yelled as the other gunmen removed their guns and aimed them at him.

Ashley quickly took off running. When she reached the bathroom door, she looked back and witnessed her father's head get blown off. After Randy was already dead, the gunmen pumped his body with a dozen more bullets just for wasting their time. Tears slid down Ashley's face as she took off out the men's room never looking back.

The leader searched Randy's dead body for what he was looking for and when he came up empty it just pissed him off even more. "He must of gave it to the little girl. Find her and bring her to me!" he ordered as he watched the rest of the gunmen exit the restroom in search of the little girl.

Ashley ran through the mall blindly. She had no clue where to go or what to do without her father. All she knew was that someone murdered her father and those same men were now after her trying to kill her. As Ashley ran through the mall she spotted a mall security guard standing by a sneaker store trying to rap to a Spanish woman who was pushing a stroller.

"Help! Help!" Ashley yelled as she ran up to the security guard. "They just killed my father and now they trying to kill me!" she said out of breath.

"Whoa, whoa, whoa, slow down for a second," the security guard said smiling down at the little girl that stood before him. "Now who's after you?"

"Some men with guns!" Ashley told him, but for some reason the guard wasn't taking her serious.

"Where are your parents?" the security guard asked with a cheesy smile. Seeing that the security guard wasn't going to be any help, Ashley took off running again.

"Crazy ass kid," the guard spat, until he saw four men running in his direction. "Hey!" he yelled with authority. "No running in the mall!"

"Oh I'm so sorry sir. I was just trying to find my daughter. She ran away," the gunman lied.

"I just saw her run that way," the security guard said pointing in the direction that the little girl had ran.

"Thank you so much," the gunman said as he fired two bullets into the guard's stomach and laughed as the security guard crumbled down to the floor.

Ashley continued running even after she heard two loud thunderous shots go off that sent the entire mall into a frenzy. A mini stampede broke out. Ashley smartly did her best to blend in with the crowd in an attempt to get away from the gunmen without getting noticed. Ashley saw a door to her right with a big sign over the top that read **EXIT**. She quickly went through the door and it lead to a set of stairs. Ashley ran down the stairs looking back over her shoulders. She continued to run until she crashed into someone.

"Are you okay?"

Ashley looked up and saw a woman with blonde hair and a pair of dark shades covering her eyes standing before her.

"Please help me," Ashley cried. "They killed my father and now they're trying to kill me," she said to the woman.

"Who's trying to kill you?"

Before Ashley could answer, the staircase door busted open and a man with a mean looking scowl on his face started heading down the stairs in an aggressive manner.

The woman with the blonde hair quickly stationed the little girl behind her to keep her out of harm's way. "Hey what's going on here?" she asked the man with her hands raised in surrender.

"Bitch!" the gunman growled as he pulled a 9mm from the small of his back, cocked it, and aimed it at the blonde haired woman's forehead. "Turn around and leave before you get your head blown off!" he threatened while still walking.

Without warning the woman with the blonde hair slapped the gunman's hand, sending the gun flying in the air. She swiftly moved behind him and threw him in a chokehold catching the gun with her free hand. Before the gunman got a chance to say a word, she pulled the trigger sending his brains flying out the back of his skull. She then tossed the gunman's lifeless body down the stairs as if it was a piece of trash. The sound of the staircase door busting open again grabbed her attention. Up at the top of the steps she spotted three men who had entered the staircase all carrying guns.

The woman with the blonde hair raised the 9mm and fired off three shots in a rapid succession. Seconds later three bodies toppled down the steps awkwardly.

The woman with the blonde hair turned to Ashley and extended her hand. "I'm Angela, come with me if you want to live."

Ashley looked down at all the dead bodies, then back up at the woman with the blonde hair, and reluctantly took her hand.

1

HARD TO KILL

The leader of the pack entered the staircase and immediately pulled his .45 from his holster when he spotted four of his comrades sprawled out dead lying lifelessly on the steps. He pulled out his cell phone and made a quick call. "Keep your eyes open it looks like the little girl has got some help. Shoot on site. I repeat, shoot on sight," he said and then ended the call. After he ended his call, the man with the beard stepped out the staircase and into the parking lot. His eyes immediately scanned from left to right as he moved swiftly through the lot until he spotted a woman with blonde hair shutting the back door to her car. It was something about the woman with the blonde hair that didn't sit right with the man with the beard.

"Excuse me ma'am!" he called out, but the woman kept on moving as if she didn't hear him. "Ma'am! Ma'am!" he called out moving faster towards the vehicle. When he made it a few feet away from the vehicle, he saw the little girl he was looking for. She looked back at him through the back window. Without thinking twice he raised his gun, aimed it at her head, and pulled the trigger; taking out the whole back window. At first the man with the beard was going to let the little girl live; that was until he saw his dead comrades laid out in the staircase.

Angela threw the car in reverse and stomped down on the gas.

Scrrrrrr!!!!

"Keep your head down," Angela said in a calm tone as shattered glass rained down on top of Ashley's head. She looked up and saw a man with a thick rugged beard running full speed towards the car. Seconds later bullets rained through the front windshield leaving holes the size of gulf balls.

With the car still in reverse, Angela grabbed the 9mm from her lap and returned fire right from the front seat causing the gunman with the beard to duck and dodge to keep from taking an unwanted bullet. Angela tossed the gun back down on her lap and looked out the shattered back window as she tried to steer her and little girl to safety. She didn't know who these men were or how many of them there were out there.

Angela made flying through the parking lot in reverse look easy. In a flash, she stomped down on the brakes and cut the wheel hard to the left causing the car to fishtail sending her body crashing into the door. She then swiftly threw the gear in drive and gunned the engine. "Keep your head down," she said over her shoulder. Before Angela could make it out of the parking lot, she spotted another gunman up ahead.

Without warning, the gunman opened fire on the vehicle that headed straight for him. Angela kept her head low and kept her foot on the gas. The vehicle ran dead into the gunman sending his head crashing through the front windshield. His body did several flips and summersaults through the air and then violently came crashing down on the concrete.

Angela looked back in the back seat and saw a scared Ashley looking up at her. "Just keep your head down and you're going to be fine." As soon as the words left her lips Angela heard a loud thump on the roof of her car. Seconds later a gloved hand shot through the driver's door window shattering the glass and grabbed Angela forcefully by the throat. Angela quickly reached down on her lap, grabbed the 9mm, raised it, and fired off four shots up into the roof of the car. Immediately the hand that was wrapped around her throat released its grip.

Ashley sat in the back seat and watched as the dead body slid awkwardly off the roof of the car. She wasn't too sure of what was going on, but she was thankful for the stranger with the blonde hair who had come to her rescue.

Angela cut the wheel hard to the right and then quickly stomped down on the brakes when she saw a parked car up ahead blocking the exit. Four gunmen hopped out the car all holding automatic weapons.

Angela smoothly slid out the front seat of the car, moved towards the back door, and snatched Ashley out of her seat. They moved swiftly between all the parked cars until they reached a pickup truck. "Hide under here," Angela whispered as she helped Ashley hide under the pickup truck. "I'll be back for you in a second."

Ashley remained quiet and replied with a simple scared head nod, but her eyes begged Angela not to leave her.

"I'll be back. I promise," Angela said as she removed a silenced .380 from her shoulder holster and quickly moved along through the parking lot.

The first gunman never knew what hit him. A throwing knife penetrated his rib cage from behind, piercing his heart causing him to slither down to the ground bleeding. *"One down and three more to go,"* Angela said to herself as she crept through the parking lot in search of the next gunman.

The next gunman stood near a parked car fumbling around in his jacket for his cell phone when a silenced .380 slug blew through his skull fragmenting on impact, and sending several chunks of lead shredding through his cerebrum. He never knew he was dying, he'd merely stopped being alive. His stay on earth ended before his body even hit the pavement.

Angela moved through the parking lot with the quietness of a cat. The third gunman stood with his back to her looking for any signs of movement in the opposite direction. A woman's hand quickly covered his mouth as a knife was plunged down into the side of his neck.

The last gunman moved throughout the parking lot in a low crouch. He didn't know who the blonde hair woman was, but the one thing he did know was that she was extremely dangerous. He took one more step and then froze up like a statue when he felt the cold steel of a pistol being pressed to the back of his head.

"Why are y'all after the girl?" Angela asked placing the final gunman in a choke hold.

"She has something that belongs to my boss."

"Who's your boss?"

"Names aren't important," the gunman growled. "What's important is that you know that you're going to die when my boss finds out about..."

A bullet to the gunman's head silenced him forever.

Ashley lay on the cold concrete floor underneath the truck. Something inside of her was telling her to try and make a run for it, but fear kept her frozen still. She almost shit her pants when she felt a hand grab a hold of her ankle. Ashley fixed her mouth to scream until she looked and saw that the hand belonged to the woman with the blonde hair.

"Come on we gotta go," Angela said as she rushed Ashley over towards the empty vehicle that the gunmen rode in. Once they were inside the vehicle, the tires burnt rubber as they peeled out of the parking lot.

2

HERE COMES

TROUBLE

Mr. Clarke sat in his office listening to the man with the beard explain to him what went wrong. He was pissed off, but did his best to remain calm. "So please explain to me how a man and a twelve year old child managed to escape several men who call themselves killers?"

"Sir, Randy wasn't a problem and neither was the twelve year old child."

"Then what was the problem?" Mr. Clarke asked with a raised brow.

"This woman came out of nowhere; some woman with blonde hair and dark sunglasses. Whoever this woman was, she was a professional," the man with the beard explained.

"You said the woman had blonde hair and dark shades?" Mr. Clarke repeated with a worried look on his face. There was only one woman he knew who fit that description. He quickly turned on his computer and pulled up a picture of Angela and then turned the monitor towards the man with the beard. "Is this the woman from the mall?"

The man with the beard looked closely at the monitor and instantly his face turned into a frown. "Yeah that's her. Who is she?"

"Her name is Angela, but the underworld knows her as The Teflon Queen!" Mr. Clarke announced with a look of stress plastered across his face. He knew that if The Teflon Queen was now in the picture that things were sure to get messy. "Fuck! I need that thumb drive!"

"Sir if you don't mind me asking," the man with the beard said looking from the computer screen to Mr. Clarke. "What's on that disk, sir?"

Mr. Clarke looked at the man with the beard like he had lost his mind. "That's none of your concern. Your only concern should be to get that thumb drive back to me as soon as possible!"

"Will do sir, but I may need a few more men because whoever this Teflon lady is she's good," the man with the beard said.

"No! I'm going to have to call in some professionals for this one. No disrespect, but Angela will dismantle you and all of your men," Mr. Clarke said.

"Who'd you have in mind?" the man with the beard asked.

"Mr. & Mrs. Chambers," Mr. Clarke announced with a sinister smirk on his face. Frank Chambers and Kate Chambers were a brutal assassin team. They were a husband and wife who loved to hurt and inflict pain on their targets. Wherever they went, a big nasty blood trail was sure to follow.

The man with the beard cracked a smile. "Is this Teflon Queen lady that good?"

"Would I be calling Mr. & Mrs. Chambers if she wasn't?"

"Well we have a tracker on the car that she and the little girl hopped in so it shouldn't be hard for Mr. & Mrs. Chambers to track her down," the man with the beard explained.

"Music to my ears," Mr. Clarke said running his hands together greedily.

3

INVESTIGATION

Detective Washington walked through the mall parking lot with a disgusted look on his face. He couldn't believe that someone would put so many innocent lives at risk. He remembered when it used to be safe to walk through the mall with your family. He planned on tracking down whoever was responsible for this carnage and by any means necessary. "What do we have?"

A uniform officer handed him a folder. "Looks like we have a missing girl by the name of Ashley Brown, last seen with this woman," he said opening the folder and pulling out a picture of a woman with blonde hair and sunglasses on.

"Angela better known as The Teflon Queen," Detective Washington said out loud. "A well-known assassin wanted by every agency out there. This is a woman with no remorse for human life. Yeah, I know all about her."

"Well little Ashley was last seen with Angela and her father Randy Brown was found dead in the men's room," the officer announced. "I'm not sure what a wanted assassin would want with a little girl, sir."

"Me either, but I promise you I'm going to find out," Detective Washington said to himself.

***

Angela ditched the car on an empty street as her and Ashley hopped in a cab and headed to a motel a few blocks away. Once inside the room, Ashley sat on the bed with a nervous and scared look on her face.

"Hungry?"

Ashley shook her head no.

"Sleepy?"

Ashley shook her head no again.

"Umm do you have any idea why all of those men with guns were after you back there?" Angela asked helping herself to a seat on the bed next to the little girl.

Ashley was about to tell the stranger about the thumb drive that her father had given her, but his words played over and over again in her head. *"No matter what happens, you keep this with you at all times and don't show it to no one and I mean no one!"* After remembering what her father said to her, Ashley lied. "No,

I have no idea." She badly wanted to show Angela the thumb drive especially after the lady had saved her life, but instead she followed her father's instructions.

"I don't understand why trained men with guns would want to kill an innocent child," Angela said out loud. "Were your parents into something illegal?" she asked. "Maybe owed someone some money?"

Ashley shrugged. "I don't know."

"Okay, don't worry about it. I'll find out and get to the bottom of this. You just get you some rest."

"Can you take me to my mommy?" Ashley asked.

Angela paused for a second. "Ummmm, sure get you some rest and we'll talk about it when you wake up." Angela didn't have the heart to tell the little girl that, that would be the next place that the killers would be heading if they hadn't gotten there already so Angela lied.

"Here let me get you something to drink," Angela walked over to the small refrigerator, popped open a Pepsi and poured it into a cup, in her other hand she discreetly crushed up a sleeping pill and sprinkled it into the cup. "Here you go," she said as she watched Ashley down the entire cup.

"What time are we going to see my mommy?" Ashley asked as she lay back on the bed.

"Do you know your address?"

"Yes," Ashley replied as she jotted her address down on the small note pad that laid on the night stand.

"After your nap," Angela replied. She was still stuck on the question of why would trained armed gunmen want to kill a child and at of all places, a mall. She had a million questions with no answers. Angela looked over and saw little Ashley sleep with her mouth open. She then quickly grabbed her jacket and headed out the door.

***

Angela crept through the back yard of a nice looking brick house. She picked the lock to the back door and entered the house with her weapon drawn. From the kitchen she could hear the T.V. at a high volume. Angela eased her way to the living room where she found a woman sitting in front of the screen watching CNN.

"Turn that TV off!" Angela barked startling the woman.

The woman in front of the TV did as she was told. "What's this all about?"

"Your daughter and why are there men trying to kill her?"

"Ashley! Where is she?" the woman blurted out.

"She's safe," Angela assured her. "Now I'm going to ask you this again. Why are there men trying to kill her?"

"My husband who is Ashley's father worked for some real bad men. I never asked what he was involved in because it wasn't my place and honestly I didn't really want to know," the woman explained. "My husband was killed in the mall and I'm just thankful that you saved my daughter." She paused for a second. "On the news they're saying that you kidnapped her, but I knew that wasn't true. I know if it wasn't for you that my daughter would be dead right along with her father"

"These people that your husband worked for, who are they?" Angela pressed.

"I don't know," the woman replied. "But once or twice I did over hear him say the name Clarke or Mr. Clarke."

"Okay well I have your daughter and she's in one piece," Angela said. "I can bring her to you if you like so you..."

"No!" the woman snapped cutting Angela off. "These men that killed my husband, they're after her for a reason. I can't protect her," she said as tears began to run down her face. "Please take care of my baby for me until all of this is over."

"Listen lady," Angela began. "I would like to help you out, but I know nothing about looking after a child and I wouldn't even know where to start."

"Please!" the woman begged. "Those men that killed my husband are still out there and they want something that my daughter has."

"What could she have that they could possibly want?"

"I have no idea. My husband must of given her something, maybe."

"Or maybe the men that killed him wants his whole family dead," Angela pointed out.

"Maybe, but I'm willing to die in order for my daughter to live to see another day," the woman said meaning every word she spoke. "Please keep her and look after her for me.... Please..."

"She been asking for you," Angela told her.

"Here take down my number," the woman said scribbling a number down on a small piece of paper. "Have her call me tonight and I'll explain everything to her myself." She handed Angela the piece of paper with her number written on it. "And thank you so much," she said as she grabbed Angela and gave her a bear hug. "Please protect my baby!"

"I'll do my best," Angela said and like that she was gone.

4

BAD NEWS

A black sleek B.M.W pulled up in front of Mr. Clarke's mansion. The driver killed the engine and stepped out in an all black tailored suit with black leather gloves on his hands. Frank Chambers had a no nonsense look on his face as usual and one with a trained eye could tell that two automatic weapons rested under each one of his arm pits. He was a Caucasian man with blue eyes and a buzz cut. He quickly walked over to the passenger's door and opened it.

Kate Chambers stepped from the B.M.W with a slick looking smirk on her face. She too was dressed in all black. She sported a tailored suit and on her feet were a pair of rubber bottom classy looking dress shoes. It was rumored that all of Mr. and Mrs. Chambers gear was bullet proof.

Kate was a Japanese woman with long silky jet black hair and a slim frame. It was rumored that out of the two she was known for being the loose cannon. Her gun of choice was two twin baby tech-9's.

The couple walked up to the front door and before they could knock or ring the bell, the maid had already opened it.

"Right this way, please. Mr. Clarke is expecting you two," the maid said as she escorted the two killers down a long hallway and around the corner until they finally reached Mr. Clarke's office.

Frank was the first to enter the office followed by his wife. Behind an oak wood desk sat Mr. Clarke.

"So glad you two made it here safely," Mr. Clarke said with a smile.

"What's the situation looking like?" Frank asked getting straight down to business. From how Mr. Clarke's voice sounded on the phone, he knew whatever the job was it had to be important.

"Well it's quite simple," Mr. Clarke began. "Something that belongs to me was taken and I want it back."

"What was taken?" Kate asked.

"That's not important. What is important is that you get it back for me. I'm paying good money so I'm expecting y'all to get the job done," Mr. Clarke said looking at the husband and wife's face for a reaction. "What I need y'all to retrieve for me is most likely going to be on a disc or thumb drive. It was stolen by one of my former employees. He's no longer with us, but somehow he managed to slip the disc or thumb drive to his daughter before he was gunned down." He paused for a second.

"So you mean to tell me that your men couldn't track down a little girl and get your disc back?" Frank asked with a raised brow.

Mr. Clarke chuckled. "Here's where the problem comes in. While my men were in pursuit of the little girl, this woman came out of nowhere and killed all of my men and helped the little girl escape," he explained with an embarrassed look on his face. "This woman is looking like she's going to be a problem, so I need you two to kill this woman and the girl and bring me back my disc."

"What's this woman's name?" Frank asked curiously.

"Angela!"

"The Teflon Queen?" Kate asked with a serious look on her face. She had heard plenty of stories of how the great Teflon Queen had destroyed plenty of lives and always managed to live to tell about it.

Mr. Clarke nodded his head up and down. "This isn't going to be a problem is it?"

"No I assure you that Angela won't be a problem," Frank said with a smirk. "No disrespect but we ain't The White Shadow!"

"They say that Angela is hard to kill," Mr. Clarke said.

"Well we'll have to see about that now won't we," Kate said aggressively. "We'll get the job done."

"For two million y'all better."

"Correction," Frank said. "The price just jumped from two million to three million. Half up front and the other half when the job is done." He knew that whatever was on that disc had to be well worth over 3 million dollars and he also knew that taking down The Teflon Queen wouldn't be a walk in the park. "That's the new price and it's nonnegotiable."

"Deal," Mr. Clarke said reluctantly. "Just make sure I get my disc back." He reached in his desk drawer and removed a photo of little Ashley along with a small piece of paper. "Here's what the little girl looks like and her address. My men had a tracker on the car that Angela stole from the scene." He reached down in his pocket and tossed Frank a small device that showed him exactly where the car was parked.

"I better receive a transfer in my account within the next hour," Frank said as him and his wife got up and made their exit.

5

NEW GUN IN TOWN

Kate hopped out of the B.M.W and walked straight up to the front door of the address that Mr. Clarke had given her. She knocked on the door, took a step back, and waited for an answer. Seconds later, the sound of the lock being unlocked could be heard followed by a middle-aged woman peeking her head out of the door.

"Yes may I help?" the woman asked.

"Yes are you the mother of Ashley Brown?"

"Yes I am. Is there a problem?" the woman asked.

"I just have a few questions to ask you," Kate said walking inside the house without an invitation. "Are you in the house alone?"

"Ummmm, and who are you again?" Ashley's mother asked. "Are you with the FBI?"

Kate spun around and back slapped Ashley's mother across the face like she was a simple whore. "Where's your daughter?"

Ashley's mother held the side of her face with a shocked look. She quickly went to run out the back door, but the site of Frank erased that thought from her mind.

Kate roughly grabbed Ashley's mother by the hair and tossed her down to the floor. Like magic a sharp knife with a four inch blade appeared in her hand. "Last time I'm going to ask you."

"I don't know where she is," Ashley's mother pleaded. "She's only a child. What do y'all want with her?"

Kate grabbed a handful of Ashley's mother's hair, lifted her head back, and jammed the knife deep into her throat. She watched as the woman died right there and blood ran down her black leather glove.

Frank walked over to the entertainment system and grabbed a framed picture of Ashley and her mother. He tossed the picture frame down to the floor and removed the photo, folded it, and stuck it down in his pocket. A recent photo of the child would be of some help when they ran into Angela and the child. He pulled out the device that showed him where the car that Angela had stolen was located. "Come on. We have to get moving."

***

Angela sat at the edge of the bed trying to figure out how she was going to handle the weird and strange situation that she found herself in. In her hand she held an empty clip. She had been filling up as many extra clips as she could. For some strange reason she had a feeling that she was going to need as many bullets as she could get her hands on.

"I'm hungry," Angela heard a voice behind her say. She turned around and saw little Ashley sitting up in the bed with a nervous look on her face.

"Hey you; I was wondering when you were going to wake up," Angela said with a smile. She didn't know the first thing about taking care of a child. The first thing she wanted to do was make Ashley feel safe and comfortable. "What would you like to eat?"

"Denny's," Ashley answered quickly.

"How about we order some food?" Angela suggested. "I'm not too sure if it's safe for us to leave the room."

"But I want Denny's," Ashley whined.

Immediately Angela realized that Ashley had no clue of the amount of trouble that she was in or the danger that lied ahead. So she tried a different approach. "How about we order take out today and then go to Denny's tomorrow. How does that sound?"

"I guess so," Ashley said with a sad puppy look on her face. After looking at her face for a few seconds, Angela broke down. "Go and get dressed." She knew them leaving the room was a risky move, but how could she tell a face like that no.

Angela grabbed an old baseball cap and put it on Ashley's head. "Here, keep this on so it'll be hard to recognize you just in case someone is out there looking for you," she said with a smile. She didn't have the heart to inform her that both of their faces were all over the news. Once Ashley was dressed, her and Angela headed out to Denny's.

6

DENNY'S

Frank pulled up beside the car that Angela had stolen and was last seen in. It took him less than two minutes to search the entire vehicle from top to bottom. "It's clean," he said as he slid back behind the wheel and pulled off. Mr. & Mrs. Chambers cruised through the area alert and on point. They knew that Angela and the little girl couldn't be but so far from here, especially since they had no clue that the vehicle that they stole had a tracker on it.

"This Teflon chick has no clue what she's up against," Kate said in a low whisper.

"Patience my queen," Frank said as he parked across the street from a low key looking hotel.

"Why did we stop?"

"My gut is telling me this is where Angela and the girl are staying," Frank said staring at the motel as if he could see through the walls.

"So what you want to stake out here for a while and see if they turn up?" Kate asked.

"Nah... We'll come back here if we turn up empty," Frank said as he pulled back out into traffic. As the two cruised the streets, Frank quickly stomped down on the brakes and pulled over towards the curb.

"What's wrong!?" Kate asked as her hand shot towards her firearm.

Frank quickly reached down in his pocket, removed the photo of Ashley and her mother, and examined it. Then he passed it to his wife. Kate looked at the picture closely and then a small smile spread across her face. "I mean, I think it's worth a try."

The photo was a photo of Ashley and her mother sitting in a booth in Denny's smiling brightly. Frank had stopped the B.M.W directly across the street from a Denny's restaurants. He quickly pulled into the restaurant's parking lot and killed the engine.

Mr. & Mrs. Chamber both slipped ear pieces in their ears before exiting the B.M.W.

Frank stepped foot in the restaurant and immediately his eyes quickly searched each face. His eyes stopped when they landed on a woman with shades on indoors and a child who sported a baseball cap that blocked part of its face. The baseball cap was low and it was hard for him to tell if the child was a boy or a girl. "Two tangos match the description at 3 o'clock," he said in a light whisper. His words registered in Kate's earpiece.

She quickly glanced in that direction without making it obvious. "Hard to tell," she replied.

"Hi, welcome to Denny's. Two?" the hostess asked like she loved working at the restaurant for tips.

"Yes and we'd like a booth please."

"Sure, right this way," the hostess said as she escorted the couple to a vacant booth. "Is this okay?"

"This is perfect. Thank you," Frank replied with a charming smile. Once they were seated, they discreetly looked over at the woman with the dark shades on and the child trying to see if they had located their targets.

"You think that's them?" Kate asked.

"Hard to tell, but I think so," Frank replied. "I'm about to make a move."

"No. I got this one," Kate said. "Just cover me."

"Got you," Frank said as he removed a 9mm from his holster, cocked it, and passed it to his wife under the table. He knew if she pulled out the tech-9, it would draw too much attention.

***

"Thank you," Angela said politely as the waitress sat their food down on the table. "You sure you going to be able to eat all that?"

Ashley nodded her head up and down with a smile on her face. "I told you I was hungry," she laughed.

Angela hated to admit, but she was kind of enjoying Ashley's company. This was definitely something different.

"I bet you I can eat all this food in three minutes," Ashley challenged with a grin.

Angela looked down at Ashley's full plate. "You gon eat all that in three minutes? No way!"

"Wanna bet?"

"No. What if you choke?" Angela said laughing. "Then what?"

"I'm not going to choke," Ashley said. "Me and my dad used to do this all the time."

"That's a lot of food. I don't think you can eat all that in three minutes."

"Okay well if I do, then you have to take me to get some ice cream," Ashley said.

"And if you don't?"

"Pick something."

"Okay if you don't eat all the food in three minutes, you won't complain about us being in the room all day."

"Bet," Ashley said sticking out her pinky. Angela looked at her pinky with a confused look on her face.

"It's not a bet unless we lock pinkies," Ashley said with a smile as she held out her pinky.

"Bet," Angela said as she locked pinkies with Ashley. "Okay you can start eating.... Now!"

Immediately Ashley dug down and began to devour her food. The site of the little girl eating her food like a savage brought a smile to Angela's face. As Angela watched Ashley eat her food, she looked up and noticed a white man and a Japanese woman acting as if they weren't watching her and Ashley's every move. Angela spotted them as soon as they entered the restaurant. Everything about them screamed trouble; from the way they walked, even down to the clothes that they wore.

"All done!" Ashley announced with her jaws filled with food.

Angela looked down at her watch. "Two minutes and thirty seconds."

"Told you I could do it," Ashley smiled.

"Drink some juice so you don't choke. Then I need you to come with me to the bathroom," Angela said with her tone changing from friendly to serious.

"Is something wrong?" Ashley asked with a nervous look on her face.

"No," Angela replied as she rose up from her seat, grabbed Ashley's hand, and escorted her to the woman's bathroom. Once inside the bathroom, Angela quickly checked to make sure that they were in there alone. She then rushed over towards the window and opened it. "Listen, I'm going to need you to hide in this last stall until I tell you to come out. Understand?"

Ashley nodded her head up and down. She didn't know what was going on, but she knew something was definitely about to go down.

"If anything happens, I want you to jump out this window and find someone that can call the police for you. You understand?"

Ashley nodded her head up and down.

"Good! Now go hide in the stall," Angela told her.

***

Kate watched closely as the woman with the dark shades and child got up and entered the bathroom. She waited fifteen seconds before she got up and headed in the direction of the restroom.

Once Kate entered the restroom, Frank got up and walked over towards the restroom and stood outside to make sure no one entered or exited.

Kate entered the restroom and immediately she spotted the woman in the dark shades standing at the sink washing her hands. Her eyes quickly scanned the entire bathroom. The child was nowhere in sight and the window was left wide open. *"The little girl must of jumped out the window,"* Kate said to herself as she walked over towards the sink next to the woman with shades and pretended like she was brushing imaginary dusk off of her suit jacket.

Kate removed a rubber band from her pocket and placed her long hair in a neat ponytail as the woman with the shades began to dry her hands off with a few paper towels. "Angela right?" Kate said in an attempt to catch the woman off guard. The unexpected look that the woman with the shades gave her, told her that she was indeed no other than the so called Teflon Queen.

With the quickness of a rattle snake, Kate snatched a 9mm from the small of her back and pointed it towards Angela.

On point Angela caught Kate's wrist causing the fire arm to discharge by accident. She bent Kate's wrist backwards causing the gun to drop and slid up under the stall.

Kate launched her head forward, breaking Angela's nose with a vicious head butt. She gripped Angela's throat with one hand and shoved her head back into the mirror with so much force that it shattered on impact. Kate threw another punch, but Angela weaved it and landed a hard left hook to Kate's ribs.

The two assassins then squared off in the middle of the bathroom. Angela surprised Kate by launching herself at her face leading with her elbow. She felt a satisfying connection with her jaw. The blow dropped Kate right where she stood and would have knocked out many of men. Thinking the fight was over, Angela got ready to head over to the stall when out of nowhere her legs were swept from under her and she fell backwards. Kate had sweep-kicked her and she hadn't reacted in time. Realizing her error, Angela went with her momentum and rolled breaking her fall as best she could. The pain from the impact shot up her side as she landed on the hard bathroom floor, but she ignored the pain and quickly shot back to her feet.

Angela stood to her feet and then suddenly a blinding flash of pain spiked up her leg from where Kate's razor sharp knife had made contact with her leg.

Kate rushed her, but Angela easily blocked the upward sweep of the knife and leveled a brutal strike to Kate's throat. Her free hand clutched at her windpipe and with the other hand the two woman fought for control of the knife.

Outside the bathroom Frank stood by the door with an unsure look on his face. He didn't know exactly what was going on inside the bathroom, but he could hear what sounded like a good fight taking place in his ear piece. "Thirty seconds and I'm coming in there!"

As the two woman fought over the knife, Kate could hear Frank's voice coming in through her ear piece.

"Are you okay? What's going on in there?" She heard him ask with concern in his voice. As the two woman continued to fight over the knife, Kate saw Ashley step out the last stall holding her 9mm in her hand with a nervous look on her face.

"Shoot her!" Angela yelled. "Ashley shoot her!"

Ashley held the gun in a two handed grip. She didn't have a clear shot at Kate. Besides her hands were trembling so bad that if she did take the shot, it was possible that she may of shot Angela by accident. Ashley stood there with the gun in her hand as she watched the two women fight for their lives. Without warning the bathroom door came busting open and in walked

Frank. Not knowing what else to do, Ashley aimed the gun at the man, closed her eyes, and fired off two shots.

Boom! Boom!

Frank quickly jumped back out of the bathroom as two bullets landed in the wall inches away from his head. The two loud gunshots sent the entire restaurant into a frenzy. Diners ran and stepped on one another in an attempt to get out of the restaurant alive.

Frank smiled as he removed a smoke grenade from his belt, pulled the pin, and tossed it inside the bathroom. He pulled his other 9mm from his holster as he heard the smoke grenade explode. On a silent count of three Frank entered the bathroom with his gun drawn. At first it was difficult for him to see but after a second his eyes began to adjust to the smoke. "Baby where are you?" he said in a light whisper as he inched further and further inside the bathroom with his pistol aimed straight ahead.

"The two tangos jumped out the window. I went after them on foot. Get the car, pull around, and try to cut them off!" Kate's voice cracked through his ear piece. Immediately Frank took off and headed for the car.

***

Detective Washington sat in his unmarked car when he got the call about a shooting at a local Denny's restaurant that wasn't too far from where he was. "Shit!" he cursed as he gunned the engine and rushed towards the restaurant. His mission was to stop as many innocent people from getting shot as possible. If he had to take a wild guess, he was sure that The Teflon Queen was somewhere in the area and had something to do with this madness.

Before Detective Washington reached the restaurant he stomped down on the brakes just barely missing a woman and a small child who ran out into the middle of the street. Next a Japanese looking woman ran across the street brandishing a fire arm. Detective Washington quickly hopped out his car and removed his Glock from the holster. "Freeze!"

The Japanese woman spun around with a Tech-9 in her hand. Without warning she opened fire.

Detective Washington quickly dove over the hood of his car as the loud sound of bullets ricocheting and pinging off the body of his car sounded off loudly. "Shit!" he cursed as he quickly called in for back up.

***

Angela grabbed Ashley's hand, when she heard the loud sound of gunfire erupt behind them in several short burst. She quickly ran towards the first car she saw and fired a bullet through the passenger side of the windshield as a warning shot. "Outta the car now!" she yelled with a look on her face that said if the driver didn't comply she wouldn't hesitate to shoot him. The driver quickly hopped out of the car and took off in a sprint.

"Come on!" Angela said as she hopped behind the wheel and watched as Ashley hopped in the back seat. "You know the routine; head down" she said as she stomped down on the gas pedal. As Angela sped away from the scene she saw the Japanese woman began to chase after the car, but with each second that passed the Japanese woman's image began to shrink smaller and smaller.

"Who were those people?" Ashley asked peeking her head up from the back seat.

"I have no idea and I don't want to find out," Angela said as she swerved through traffic like a maniac. She was trying to put as much distance between them and the killers as possible. What bothered her the most was that she was clueless of who the two killers were and she wasn't sure if there were even more of them out there. "Why are these people after you?" Angela asked glancing back at Ashley through the rearview mirror.

"I don't know," Ashley lied. Her father had given her specific instructions not to tell a soul about the thumb drive.

"Listen Ashley I need you to think really, really, hard. These killers are after you for a reason and I need to know what's going on so I can protect you."

Ashley let Angela's words sink in for a second and just as she was about to spill the beans, several bullets ripped through the back windshield. Shattered glass showered down on top of Ashley's head as she felt the car swerve from left to right.

"Keep your head down!" Angela yelled as she stomped down on the gas. In the rearview mirror she spotted a black sleek B.M.W. speeding up on them from the side. Angela took a closer look and spotted the Japanese woman hanging halfway out the passenger side window with a machine gun clutched in her grip.

Angela quickly grabbed the silenced .380 from off her lap, stuck her arm out the window and fired off five shots in rapid succession. The five shots caused the B.M.W. to slow its pace a little and that gave Angela a little time to come up with some type of plan.

Several more bullets from the Japanese woman's gun tore through the car's frame and blew out the front tires. The tire blowout caused the car to swerve uncontrollably.

"Aw shit!" Angela cursed as she gripped the steering wheel as the car took flight and left the road. The car crashed through a series of smaller trees before coming to rest at a larger one with a big bang.

***

Frank quickly pulled the B.M.W over to the side of the road after witnessing Angela's car swerve recklessly off of the road and down into the woods. He wasn't the one for all the games. Frank pulled his 9mm from its holster and screwed a suppressor on the nose of the handgun and then he proceeded down into the woods with Kate in tow.

Frank spotted Angela's vehicle sitting idly in front of a big tree. The car was wrecked and the chances of someone surviving a crash like that were slim to none. He held a firm two handed grip on his pistol as he eased his way towards the vehicle. Just as he started to walk up on the car, a down pour of rain dropped down from the sky making it difficult for Frank to hear any sudden movement. He reached the driver's door and aimed the business end of his gun through the window ready to pull the trigger, but to his surprise the vehicle was empty. "It's empty," he said looking over towards Kate. A silent bullet pinged loudly inches away from Frank's face hitting the body of the vehicle. Frank and Kate immediately took cover behind the vehicle. They didn't know where Angela was, but they knew she was somewhere close by. They couldn't see her, but she could definitely see them.

"The rain is making it hard for me to see," Kate said as she slapped a fresh clip in her Tech-9.

"We'll just have to smoke her out," Frank told her. "On the count of three!"

At the count of three, Kate sprang from behind the car and opened fire into the trees while Frank raised his head just above the vehicle looking for any type of movement.

Kate swept her arms back and forth as she held her finger down on the trigger. While the bullets were flying Frank spotted movement from the corner of his eye.

"Target moving three o'clock!" Frank said as he took off in that direction. He trotted at a cautious pace not wanting to run into a bullet. As Frank moved, suddenly his legs were swept from up under him sending him crashing down flat on his back. He hit the ground hard and raised his gun to fire off a shot, but his hand was quickly slapped away sending the gun flying out of his hand. A knife was then jammed down into his shoulder.

Frank ignored the pain as his hand shot out and grabbed Angela by the throat. He tried to squeeze the life out of her.

Angel could feel the life being squeezed out of her. She quickly grabbed the handle of the knife and gave it a strong turn.

"Arrrgh!" Frank growled as he released his grip from around Angela's throat and snatched the knife out of his shoulder.

"Ashley run!" Angela yelled as she spotted the Japanese woman moving in their direction at a quick pace. Without thinking twice Ashley did as she was told. Fear was making her legs move faster than they had ever moved before.

Angela quickly ran and dived behind a large rock as Kate opened fire trying to take her head off.

"I got her! You go after the girl," Frank told his wife.

"Be careful," Kate said as she took off in a full sprint after the little girl.

Frank gripped the knife that he ripped from his shoulder tightly as he inched his way towards the rock that Angela hid behind. He quickly sprung around the corner with the knife in his hand ready to attack, but once again Angela was gone.

"Fuck!!!" Frank cursed as he pulled his back up weapon from the small of his back and took off in the direction he had last seen his wife running in.

***

Kate sprinted through the woods full speed until she finally caught up with little Ashley. She grabbed her by the back of her shirt and tossed her face first down into a pile of leaves. "Where is it?"

"Where's what?" Ashley faked ignorance. She was rewarded with a slap to her face for her answer.

"Where is the disk, chip, or thumb drive that your father gave you before he died?" Kate asked in a more firm tone.

"My father didn't give me anything," Ashley lied.

Smack!

She was rewarded with another slap, a back hand this time.

"Listen kid," Kate said grabbing Ashley by the collar of her shirt and jamming her Tech-9 into the child's rib cage. "One bullet from this gun will put your brains all over these bushes out here. Please don't play with me. Tell me what I need to know and I'll be on my way, but if you keep playing with me I'm going to have to hurt you," she warned.

"I wouldn't do that if I were you," a voice said from behind a tree. When Kate looked up two bullets exploded into her rib cage and back area sending her crumbling down to the ground.

Detective Washington stepped from behind the tree with a smoking .45 in his hand. He was the type to shoot first and ask questions later. "Are you okay?" he asked looking down at little Ashley.

Ashley nodded her head up and down. Detective Washington looked down at the Japanese woman who was squirming around on the ground in agony. He quickly kneeled down and hand cuffed the woman's hands behind her back. Then he called in for back up as he hurriedly escorted Ashley out of harm's way and out of the woods. He would come back for the Japanese woman later. His main priority was to get the little girl to safety.

Minutes later Frank found his wife lying face down on the ground with her hands cuffed behind her back. "You alright?" he asked as he roughly lifted Kate back up to her feet.

"I'm good. A stupid detective showed up out of nowhere," she explained as Frank rushed her through the woods before any more cops showed up.

Angela watched closely as the detective escorted Ashley out of the woods and placed her in the back of a squad car. She thought about trying to make a move on him, but seconds later there were cops all over the place. "Shit!" Angela cursed as she disappeared back into the woods.

7

WHERE'S ASHLEY

Angela stood in the motel bathroom looking at her reflection in the mirror. The discoloration on her jaw was noticeable and probably would be for a few days. She'd need to get some make-up to cover it up so as not to arouse attention. Her mind was focused on who the man and woman assassin team were. From how they moved, Angela knew that they were sure to be big trouble. The assassin team was highly skilled and had a thirst for blood, but what puzzled Angela the most was, why would hired assassins be after Ashley.

"It has to be something that they're after," Angela said to herself. While she was out, she purchased a smart phone so she picked up her phone and went straight to google and typed in the name Mr. Clarke. She knew it was a long shot but she wanted to see if any important people by that name came up in her search. Angela had remembered that Ashley's mother mentioned that's

who her husband worked for. After doing a little bit of research on Mr. Clarke, Angela found out that there was a Mr. Clarke who was into politics, but she knew that if this was the Mr. Clarke she was looking for, it was a lot more to his story than that.

On the T.V. Angela watched Detective Washington walk through several reporters and camera men refusing to answer any questions as he carried little Ashley in his arms and into the police headquarters. She quickly flipped the channel and saw that Detective Washington and little Ashley were on all of the local news stations as well as CNN. "Shit!!!" she cursed as she quickly threw on her gear and headed out the door to the police headquarters. Angela knew if she wanted to save Ashley, she would have to move fast, especially since the media had informed the entire world of Ashley's location.

8

ⒽⓊⓃⓉⒾⓃⒼ

"You alright baby?" Frank asked as he gently massaged and rubbed Kate's ribs and back area where she had been shot.

"I'm okay, just a little sore," she said as she winced in pain. "Thank God for that bullet proof fabric in our clothes."

Frank planned on making an example out of the detective that called himself saving the day. In the Medias eyes he was a hero, but in Frank's eyes he was nothing but a dead man walking. After he got done with the detective, The Teflon Queen would be next on his list. Frank hated to admit it, but Angela definitely had skills and she was proving to be a challenge.

"What you think about this Teflon chick?" Kate asked as she lay across the bed flat on her stomach.

"I'm not impressed," Frank huffed.

Kate chuckled. "Her fighting skills aren't too bad. Not the best I've seen, but not the worst either." Just like Frank, Kate too looked forward to the challenge that lied ahead. "May the best man or woman win," she said smiling.

As Frank massaged Kate's back, his hands made their way down to her plump ass and slowly pulled her hot pink thong down.

Kate quickly got in Frank's favorite position, all fours. She laid face down with her ass up while on all fours with her face buried into a pillow. Then she took both of her hands and spread her ass wide open. "Come eat this pussy!" she growled in a sexually charged voice.

Frank quickly ducked his head low and began licking on Kate's clit in a slow circular motion. He then followed up with long drawn out slurps as he worked two fingers in and out of her vagina at the same time.

"Yes that's right..." Kate moaned. "Suck on this pussy like it's yours," she growled with her voice a little muffled from her face being buried in the pillow.

Frank rolled his wife over and kissed her sloppily. When he was done, he flipped her over and put her breast and face deep into the white pillow. Kate caught her breath, got comfortable, and turned her face so she wouldn't suffocate. She was anticipating pain and pleasure. Frank positioned himself behind her, eased inside her, gripped her long hair, and stroked her hard.

He rode her, moved in deep, held on to her tightly, and filled her up. His movements were driving her insane.

"You love this dick!?" Frank asked as he slapped Kate's ass and watched as it jiggled.

"Oh my God, yes I love this dick!" Kate growled through clenched teeth.

"You want me to fuck you harder!?" Frank slapped her ass again.

"Yeeesssss, yes please fuck me harder!"

Frank made her beg. She begged for him to fuck her. He gave her longs strokes, his skin slapping loudly against hers.

"Argh!" Kate moaned loudly as her orgasm took over and had her speaking in tongues.

Frank gave Kate five more strong strokes before he exploded inside of her with a loud grunt.

"Damnnnn," Kate whispered with her eyes still closed. Her breathing was intense and her body was still slightly trembling.

The husband and wife took thirty minutes to get themselves back together before it was back to business. Kate stepped out of the bathroom fully dressed in a pants suit. The only difference between this one and the one she had on before was this one was smoke gray instead of black. Over by the bed Frank had several types of guns laid out on the bed. Kate walked up and grabbed two 16 shot 9mm's with silencers attached and stuck them down into her shoulder holsters. She then grabbed a backup .380 and slipped it in the holster on the small of her back. Next she grabbed a sheet of throwing knives and strapped it around her waist.

Frank stood with a smile on his face and watched as his wife prepared herself for battle. Kate looked up and caught Frank staring at her. "What?"

"I love you; that's what," he said smiling. "Now come on and let's go get this stupid ass kid," he said as the two exited their hotel room and hit the streets.

***

As Detective Washington walked throughout the station, he received a bunch of pats on the back and praise for rescuing little Ashley. He paid all the praise no mind. The department may have thought they scored a victory, but Detective Washington knew better. He was smart enough to know that whoever was after the little girl was still out there lurking somewhere.

"Where's the little girl?" he asked a uniform officer.

"She right there in the room sleeping. The F.B.I is on the way to come pick her up now," the officer announced.

"Motherfucking F.B.I always want to control shit," Detective Washington mumbled as he entered the holding room where little Ashley sat with a scared look on her face.

"Hey there," Detective Washington said in a soft tone as he helped himself to a seat next to Ashley. "I thought you were sleeping?"

"Can't sleep," Ashley replied.

"You can rest sweetie. There ain't no bad guys in here," Detective Washington chuckled. "Trust me, Angela won't be able to get to you while you're here. You're safe here."

"Angela is not the bad guy," Ashley told him. "She saved my life more than once."

"I know you are just a child and you may not understand, but it's best if you stay as far away from Angela as possible. She may seem like a nice lady, but the truth is, she's a very violent and dangerous person."

"You don't know her," Ashley countered. "She wouldn't hurt me."

"Are you hungry?" Detective Washington asked changing the subject. He knew Ashley was too young to understand and he didn't have the time to go back and forth with a child.

"No, I want my mother."

"I'll work on that right now," Detective Washington said as he got up and exited the room. He didn't have the heart to tell the little girl that her mother had been murdered.

9

F B I

Kate sat on the roof of a nice looking building. In front of her sat a guitar case. She snapped the case open and began to assemble the sniper rifle that sat inside. Her hands moved expertly as she assembled the rifle in two minutes flat. She sat and adjusted the high power scope.

"Black sedan carrying four tangos forty five seconds away," Frank's voice chirped into her ear piece.

"Roger that," Kate replied as she laid flat on her stomach and waited the arrival of her target. Seconds later, Kate saw an all black sedan come to a stop at a traffic light. The tints on the windows were dark, but the high powered scope helped Kate's vision. Her crosshairs landed on the driver first. Once Kate was sure she had a perfect shot, she squeezed down on the trigger. The bullet shattered the driver's window and took out the driver. The rifles stock slammed into her shoulder, but she ignored the recoil and targeted the passenger next. A split second later his brains popped out the back of his skull painting the windows red. Before the last two passengers could even figure out what was going on, Kate turned their lights out. Four head shots. "Targets down," she said as she began to break down the rifle and stick it back down in its case.

Another black sedan pulled up side by side with the F.B.I.'s sedan. Frank and one of Mr. Clarke's men hopped in F.B.I.'s sedan and pulled off quickly before anyone could catch wind of what was going on.

The sedans came to a stop two blocks away, on a quiet street. Frank quickly hopped out and undressed the four F.B.I. agents. "Here put this on," he said tossing a uniform to each one of the three men that Mr. Clarke had supplied him with. They weren't the best qualified, but they would serve a purpose. Once they all had on F.B.I. uniforms, Frank slid in the passenger seat of the sedan and ordered the driver to pull off. In his lap he loaded a 16 shot 9mm, and then placed it in his holster. Frank was sick and tired of playing this cat and mouse game. The next person that got in his way, he promised to make them regret it.

Twenty minutes later the sedan pulled up to the side entrance of the police headquarters. "Come on let's make this quick," Frank said leading the pack inside.

"F.B.I.," Frank said and flashed his badge quickly. He shoved it back down into his pocket before anyone had a chance to thoroughly inspect it. "We're here to pick up Ashley Brown," he spoke with authority.

"You guys are late," the officer at the front desk said with a slight attitude as he got up and went in the back. He returned about ten minutes later with little Ashley.

"Here she is," the officer said handing Ashley over to Frank. Frank made sure to keep his head low so the little girl wouldn't recognize him. The F.B.I. cap he wore was pulled down low almost covering his eyes. Frank and his men were getting ready to make their exit when a strong voice stopped them.

"Excuse me!" Detective Washington called from the hallway. "What's going on?"

"They're here to pick up the girl," the officer at the desk answered.

"Okay did they give you a transfer form?"

"No," the desk officer said with a dumb look on his face. He was kind of new on the job and didn't feel it was his place to question an F.B.I. agent so he kept his mouth shut.

Detective Washington stepped up. "Transfer form?" he said with his hand held out.

Frank patted his pockets as if he were looking for it then said, "Damn I must of forgotten it."

"Oh really?" Detective Washington said giving the agent a suspicious look. "And how long have you been on the force?"

"Listen I don't have time to play word games with you. Now if you'll excuse me, I have to get this girl back before my boss hands me my ass," Frank said in a convincing manner.

"Well I'm sorry, but I can't let this girl go with you unless you a transfer form," Detective Washington stated plainly. "Or either you can get your supervisor on the phone."

The two men stood there having a face off. Neither man backing down. Several officers in the department eased out into the lobby area and stood behind Detective Washington.

"Stand down!" Frank growled as he grabbed a hold of little Ashley's hand.

Detective Washington walked behind the desk and grabbed the phone. Just as he dialed the last number, he saw the agent make a move.

Frank pulled his 9mm from its holster and put a bullet right between the officer that stood behind the front desk eyes. He grabbed Ashley's wrist tighter and rushed her towards the exit as the rest of his men opened fire on the policemen, turning the police station into a mini war zone.

Frank rushed out the front door and got ready to roughly toss little Ashley in the back seat, but a barrel being pressed into the back of his head stopped him in mid-stride.

"Take another step and that'll be the last thing you do!" Angela growled as she reached around Frank's waist and removed his 9mm from his holster and then tossed it. "Ashley I want you to run as fast as you can. NOW!" she barked as she watched little Ashley take off down the street in a full sprint.

"Who hired you and what interest do you have with a child?" Angela asked with a .45 placed to the back of the man's skull.

As Frank stood there with a gun to his head, he noticed Kate's car pull up directly across the street from where he stood. "Pull the trigger!"

"Who do you work for? This is the last time I'm going to ask you," Angela snarled shoving the barrel further into the back of Frank's head.

"Fuck you!" Frank spat. Just as Angela pulled the trigger, Frank spun and swept his hand across the gun moving his head in the opposite direction just as the gun discharged.

Once Frank was out of the line of fire, Kate opened fire in Angela's direction with her MTAR. The gun rattled in her hand as empty shells popped out the side of the gun continuously.

Angela quickly took cover behind the sedan as shattered glass showered on the top of her head while bullets riddled and rocked the vehicle.

"Come on baby I got you," Kate spoke in a calm tone as her eyes scanned back and forth looking for any sign of Angela while Frank quickly made his way over the car. "You alright?"

"I'm good," Frank replied as he grabbed a 9mm from out of the car. "Take care of Angela while I go after the girl," he said as he took off in a sprint down the street.

Kate slowly eased her way over to the other side of the sedan. "Shit," she whispered when she saw that no one was behind the vehicle. She was just about to run up the block and go searching for the little girl when she heard somebody yell freeze from behind her. Kate slowly placed her MTAR on the ground and then came up quickly as she tossed a throwing knife in the direction of the voice with a slight flick of her wrist. The knife spun through the air and then landed in the center of the officer's throat. Kate chuckled as she watched the officer struggle to take his last breath. She picked up her gun from off the ground and before she could take a step, two bullets exploded in her chest dropping her off impact.

Kate looked up from the ground and saw a figure in an all black dash around a car. She used all of her strength, lifted her gun up, and fired in the direction of the figure in all black before she peeled herself off the ground and struggled back to her feet. The two bullets hurt and felt like they may have broken a bone in her chest. "Shit!"

Angela dodged between two cars and took a knee as blood ran down her shoulder like a faucet. A stray bullet from Kate's machine gun had found a home in her shoulder. Angela sucked up the pain and took off down the street in the direction that little Ashley had headed. She couldn't see Ashley but she already knew that the little girl was in trouble and needed her help.

10

SOMEBODY HELP

Little Ashley ran blindly down the street. The last thing she wanted was to get caught by the bad guys. After running for so long Ashley felt herself getting tired and short winded. Not knowing what else to do, she decided to run inside of a fast food restaurant but a woman stopped her.

"Hey slow down," the woman said with a drunken smile on her face. "Where you off to in such a hurry?"

"They're trying to kill me. I need you to help me!" Ashley said in a high pitched voice. "Do you have a phone? I need to call the police."

The drunken woman laughed loudly. "Who's trying to kill you; the Boogyman?"

"No I'm serious!"

"Where are your parents?" the drunken woman asked just as Detective Washington strolled up almost out of breath breathing heavily.

"Ashley come on we have to go!" he said in a stern tone.

"And who might you be?" the drunken woman asked as she grabbed Ashley's wrist and positioned her behind her.

"Listen woman right now is not the time!" Detective Washington said as he reached for Ashley's arm, but the drunken woman quickly slapped his hand away.

"Sir if you don't leave this girl alone, I'm going to be forced to hurt you," the drunken woman spat as she pulled a small dull looking knife from her pocket and opened it with a snap. Before Detective Washington could even make a move, the woman began screaming at the top of her lungs.

"Help! Somebody help me!" the woman screamed making a scene. "This man is trying to kidnap us! Somebody help!"

Detective Washington went in to try and take the drunken woman down when she suddenly dropped down to the ground. When he looked down, he saw blood splattered all across little Ashley's face. The drunken lady's brains were lying on the side of the curb. He quickly grabbed Ashley's hand as the two ran in a low crouch as several bullets pinged against all the parked cars that lined up on the street. Not having any other choice,

Detective Washington lead Ashley in the nearby supermarket in an attempt to keep her out of harm's way.

Detective Washington ran up to the first worker he saw. "Hey, I need you to call the cops immediately and clear this place out! Do it now!" he barked as he ran and did his best to blend in with the rest of the customers. Detective Washington had no clue what his next move was, but he knew he couldn't let anything happen to the little girl.

The store worker brushed Detective Washington off as some crazy man who was high on some good stuff and continued with what he was doing as if nothing ever happened.

Frank stood outside the supermarket and placed a fresh clip in the base of his 9mm. He also removed his back up P90 from the small of his back and then entered a few supermarkets. He was sick and tired of all the roadblocks that presented itself during this mission. Playtime was now officially over.

"Baby?" he called out. Seconds later Kate's voice cracked through his ear piece.

"Yes baby?"

"Location?"

"Headed your way. I'm hit."

"Where?" Frank asked with his voice full of concern.

"Two to the chest, but I'm okay and I'm certain that I hit that Teflon bitch!" her voice barked through Frank's ear piece.

"Copy; I'm in a supermarket. It's the only supermarket on the strip so you can't miss it," Frank said as he continued with the mission at hand. His wife was wounded, but still the mission had to go on. Frank walked cautiously through the supermarket as his eyes scanned from left to right. It was the beginning of the month so the place was packed with customers from all different races.

Frank strolled through the supermarket until a worker stood in front of him.

"Excuse me sir but I'm going to have to ask you to leave this store."

Frank swung his arm so quick that the man didn't even see him swing. The butt of his gun shattered the man's nose and sent him crashing down to the floor in agony.

Angela stepped foot in the supermarket and immediately she didn't like the situation. There were too many innocent people walking around. She quickly jogged throughout the store looking for Ashley.

Two minutes later Kate entered the supermarket with a mean scowl on her face. "Baby I'm in the supermarket. You still in here?"

"Yeah still searching for the girl. She's in here somewhere."

Kate quickly walked over to a man in a suit that looked like the manager. She grabbed him by his shirt and lunged forward landing a vicious head butt to the man's face that broke his nose. "Do you have keys to this store?" she asked as she jammed the gun into his stomach.

The manager nodded his head quickly as blood poured from his nose like a waterfall. Kate yanked the manager forcefully leading him over to the front door. "Lock this door now!" she demanded. Without thinking twice the man did as he was told. Once he was done Kate snatched the keys from his hands and fired a bullet in his stomach killing him on the spot.

Frank looked up and two men were approaching him wearing fatigues from head to toe. He figured the two men had served in the service. Without thinking twice Frank put a bullet in both men's head and kept it moving like it was nothing. The loud gun shots sent the entire store in a panic. People ran, pushed, and shoved one another in an attempt to get out of the supermarket but it was no use because everyone was trapped inside.

Angela heard the gun shots ring out throughout the supermarket and knew she would have to move fast if she planned to save Ashley. She moved cautiously throughout the store as blood trickled down from her fingers. The hole in her shoulder hurt like hell, but at the moment she had to ignore the pain. All the chaos and people running around screaming made it hard for Angela to focus on who was who. Her eyes were looking for anyone or anything that looked suspicious and out of place.

***

Detective Washington eased down an aisle taking caution steps. He didn't know what to expect from the killers, nor did he know how many of them were in the supermarket. "Hold up!" he whispered to Ashley as he spotted the Japanese woman that he had shot the other day walk pass the aisle he was in with a big gun in her hand. "Wait right here and don't move. I'll be right back," Detective Washington told her as he went after the Japanese woman.

Detective Washington stepped out the aisle and witnessed the Japanese woman shoot an innocent man in the face out of frustration. He quickly crept up on her from behind. "Drop it now!" he barked.

Frank stood a few aisles over when he heard Detective Washington's voice crackle in his ear piece informing him that his wife was in trouble. "I'm on my way," he said through his ear piece.

Kate stood in place still holding on to her machine gun.

"I said drop it!" Detective Washington repeated again moving in closer. Finally the Japanese woman did as she was told.

He moved in and forcefully grabbed Kate's arm and jerked it back in an attempt to handcuff her. In a quick motion Kate spun in the same direction using Detective Washington's momentum against him. In a blink of an eye Kate landed a hard blow to the detective's throat and then followed up with a swift kick between his legs. Detective Washington winced in pain as the blow between his legs dropped him down to his knees. He tried to aim his gun at the woman and pull the trigger, but he was quickly disarmed.

Kate grabbed the detective's wrist and bent it backwards until he released the gun. She caught the gun in mid-air before it hit the floor and pressed the barrel of the gun against the detective's forehead. Just as she went to pull the trigger a bullet exploded in her hand causing her to drop the gun she was holding. When Kate looked up, a bullet struck her right between her eyes killing her on the spot.

Detective Washington watched as the Japanese woman's body dropped down to floor. He then looked up and saw Angela headed down the aisle where he had left Ashley. Detective Washington hopped back up to his feet and snatched his backup weapon from its holster. He was about to go after Angela when Frank sprang from an aisle and opened fire on him.

Detective Washington quickly took off down the nearest aisle, not wanting to be on the receiving end of a stray bullet.

Frank was about to go after the cop when he spotted his wife laying in a pool of her own blood with a small hole between her eyes. "Nooooo," he whispered and then knelt down next to his dead wife. "Noooo baby," he sobbed as a single tear dropped from his eye. The pained look on Frank's face quickly turned into rage. He hurriedly grabbed Kate's MTAR machine gun and opened fired on anything moving. He walked from aisle to aisle killing any and everything moving. Seeing his wife lying dead on the floor caused Frank to snap. At the moment all he saw was red. Frank swept his arms from side to side killing anything moving. He let the empty clip drop from the base of his gun and quickly inserted a brand new clip and picked up right where he left off at.

Detective Washington stood in an aisle with dead bodies lying all around his feet. "Shit!" he cursed as his brain worked a hundred miles a second trying to come up with an escape plan. The longer he stood thinking, the faster his heart began to beat. Detective Washington quickly laid down on the floor and pulled several dead bodies over top of him. It was a sick plan, but at the moment he felt like this was his only option.

When Detective Washington saw Frank's boots come into plain sight, he quickly closed his eyes and played dead.

Frank walked through the supermarket in search for any sign of life with murder in his eyes and a big gun in his hand. Frank stopped short when he thought he saw movement coming from a pile of dead bodies. He started to inch his way over towards the pile of dead bodies, until the sound of broken glass erupted throughout the store from the police breaking down the front door. He then quickly made a dash for the back exit and never looked back.

***

Angela quickly crept up on a middle aged black man while he was putting a few bags in his trunk and stuck her gun into his ribs. "I need to borrow your car!" she growled. Without a word the man handed over his keys and stepped away from the car.

"Thank you," Angela said as her and Ashley hopped in the car and pulled off recklessly out into traffic. After narrowly escaping out the back door of the supermarket Angela was just happy that Ashley was still alive and now back in her custody. Now all she had to do was keep her alive and find out why everyone wanted this little girl dead.

11

DOWN ON MY LUCK

Scarface stepped foot out the county jail and inhaled the fresh air deeply. It had been three and a half weeks since he had seen the streets and to be honest he wasn't sure that this day would ever come. His mother had to put up her house as well as a few other properties that he had in her name to get him out. When the cops pulled him over they found two handguns in the glove compartment along with a tied up Mya in the trunk area of the truck. While Scarface was locked up he found out that Mya had told the police everything, from how he had shot and killed her boyfriend Tyrone, to how he assaulted and kidnapped her. She even went as far as telling the police that if they hadn't pulled his vehicle over, she wouldn't still be alive right now. The more the story unfolded the more it pissed Scarface off. It was him who begged Mya to leave him alone and even paid her a few dollars twice a week to stay away from him and Shekia. Not to mention while he was locked up he had to deal with the fact that he had just lost his sister Vicky, and the woman he loved was involved in a bad car accident. That alone would be enough to drive anybody crazy.

Scarface walked to the vehicle that awaited him curbside and hopped in the passenger seat. In the driver seat sat his most trusted friend, Black.

"Welcome home," Black said with a smile as he quickly pulled away from the jail.

"Feels good to be home," Scarface said honestly as he grabbed the bottle of peach Ciroc that rested by his feet and filled up a Styrofoam cup with half Ciroc and the other half orange juice. "What I miss?"

"Shit been all fucked up since you been gone," Black said shaking his head with a disgusted look on his face. "Ever since you got knocked, the cops been snooping around at an all-time high. They are arresting everything moving."

"Any word on that nigga Bone?" Scarface asked with fire dancing in his eyes. The entire time he was in jail he regretted involving his sister Vicky in his street beef.

"Word on the streets is that Bone and his team is out here in Miami for the weekend celebrating," Black told him.

"He's here in Miami right now?" Scarface asked with a raised voice.

Black nodded his head. "I got all our peoples trying to find out where they going to be tonight."

"I should of never sent Vicky out to New York in the first place." Scarface took a deep gulp from his cup. "What's the word on Mya?"

"Word is she is in protective custody, but a few niggaz been saying that they saw her here and there," Black said filling him in. "But I don't know how true that is, cause I heard she was seen at the liquor store the other day."

"How's Shekia?" Scarface asked. What really bothered him the most while he was locked up was that his woman was laid up in the hospital and it wasn't anything that he could do about it.

An awkward silence fell upon them before Black finally spoke. "Shekia moved out the crib and word is she staying with some new nigga."

"Some new nigga!?" Scarface echoed with his face crumbled up. "I know she ain't get a new man already. I've only been gone for three and a half weeks."

Black didn't reply. Instead he just kept his eyes on the road. He hated to have to be the one to break the news to his friend, but he had to tell him. "She probably thought that you were never coming home," he shrugged.

"You got an address on where she staying?"

Black nodded his head.

"Detour! Take me straight there," Scarface demanded. *"The nerve of this bitch, to go find another man while I'm in jail"* he thought as he watched the streets pass by in a blur.

Twenty minutes later Black parked in front of a nice looking town house. Before he could even turn the car off, Scarface was already out the car and heading towards the front door.

KNOCK! KNOCK! KNOCK!

Seconds later a white man dressed in slacks and a dress shirt with a pair of nerdy glasses on answered the door. "May I help you?" he asked politely.

"Yeah Shekia, is she here?"

"Yes but she's still recovering and I don't think she wants any visitors today, so maybe you should..."

"Fuck all that!" Scarface huffed cutting the white man off as he forced his way in the front door disregarding the man's wishes. The white man was about to try to physically throw the intruder out, but the cannon that Black shoved in his face made him have a change of heart.

"Don't make me clap fire out that ass!" Black warned as he forcefully shoved the white man through the house and down onto the couch.

Scarface walked all throughout the house until he reached the bedroom and saw Shekia sitting on the bed with her leg in a cast sitting propped up on a few pillows. "Fuck is up?" he asked barging into the bedroom.

"What are you doing here and where is Matt," Shekia asked sitting up.

"Fuck Matt!" Scarface snapped. "Fuck is you doing here and why ain't you home?"

"The last time I saw you, you kicked me out remember?" Shekia said refreshing his memory.

"Okay so we have a misunderstanding and you go get a new man, a new crib, and don't tell nobody. Then on top of that you don't even check on a nigga while he in jail?"

"First of all, we didn't have a misunderstanding," she said making air quotes with her fingers. "We had a nasty fight and you said some things that I don't think I can forgive."

"Come on baby you know I didn't mean that shit," Scarface lied. The truth was in the heat of the argument, he did in fact mean everything he said, but later he realized that he was dead wrong. He wanted to make it right, but when he tried he was too late.

"You meant it," Shekia continued. "Besides ain't you still involved with your ex Mya," she said with a hint of jealousy in her tone. "I mean that's the word on the streets."

"Listen baby the only woman I want is you. In one night my sister got murdered, my woman got in an accident, and I got locked up, and now I'm facing murder charges."

"Oh my God," Shekia said covering her mouth in shock. "What happened to Vicky?"

"Bone murdered her," he answered with his head down.

"What!?" Shekia asked looking at Scarface like he was insane. "I told you to let that stupid beef between you and Bone go and now because of you Vicky is dead!"

"I can't just let another man get away with putting his hands on you!" Scarface snapped. "Fuck that!"

"Was it worth it!?" Shekia asked. Scarface's silence was all the answer that she needed. "Come here," she said holding her arms open for a hug. Scarface slid in between her arms and hugged her tightly as if this was the last time that he would ever hug a woman.

"Who the fuck is that white nigga in the living room?"

Shekia chuckled. "Why? You jealous?"

"Don't play with me," Scarface warned.

"Calm down. He's just my home health nurse," she told him with a smile and then kissed him. "I missed you."

"I missed you too," Scarface replied as a light knock at the door grabbed his attention. He turned around and saw Black standing in the door.

"Gimme one second," he said excusing himself from Shekia.

"I just got word that this clown Bone is downtown at some new club that opened not too far away from here," Black told him. "What you wanna do? It's your call?"

Scarface paused for a brief second and then said, "we in there!"

"Umm where's Matt?" Shekia asked.

Black flashed a smirk and then said, "he sleep."

All Shekia could do was shake her head.

"I have to go take care of something real quick baby. When Matt wakes up tell him to help you pack all your shit and go back home."

"But..."

"Ain't no but's! Just do it!" Scarface said and then was out the door.

For the entire ride, Scarface was silent. For what he had planned, no talking would be necessary. For the last three and a half weeks, he had visualized what he would do to the man who murdered his sister when he finally ran into him and the outcome wasn't pretty.

"How much longer until we get there?" Scarface asked.

"About fifteen minutes," Black answered.

"A'ight step on it," Scarface said as he checked the clip on the .45 that rested on his lap. Seventeen minutes later Black pulled into club's parking lot and placed the gear in park. "What's the word?"

Scarface sat there for a second. A million thoughts ran through his mind all at once. Scenario after scenario played in his mind and all of them ended badly. "Take me back to the crib."

"Huh?" Black asked. He knew he must of heard Scarface wrong.

"Take me back to the house," Scarface repeated. After giving it some thought he realized that God had given him a second chance at life and the odds of him running up in the club and coming out alive or with his freedom were slim to none. "We'll catch him next time." He knew Black probably wouldn't understand but as long as it made sense in his mind that's all that mattered.

Black pulled out of the parking lot and did as he was told. He didn't understand why they weren't getting their hands dirty tonight, but he knew his position and played it well. "What's the plan?"

"I haven't thought of one yet," Scarface said honestly. "But just know that I'll never let that clown get away with what he did to my sister."

12

BAD TO THE BONE

Y.G.'s song *"My Nigga"* blasted loudly through the club's speakers.

Bone stood on the couch in the VIP section with a bottle in one hand and a fist full dollars in the other hand acting a fool as usual. His right hand man Mike Murder stood close by. His eyes scanned back and forth looking for any signs of trouble. Several other young shooters stood around the VIP section trying to holla at all the chicks that flooded the section.

Bone jumped down off the couch and took a long swig from his bottle when he looked up and saw a dark skin woman with a body that looked like she paid good for it sitting down staring at him. Wasting no time, Bone walked right up to the woman and stood directly in front of her purposely positioning his crotch to be directly in the woman's face and line of vision. "What's shaking baby?" he said and then took another guzzle from his bottle.

"Shit definitely not you," the chick said in an uninterested tone as she pulled out her iPhone and pretended like she was doing something important.

"So why every time I look up you looking in my mouth?" he asked in a slur.

"Nigga please," the dark skin chick said looking up at Bone like he was insane. "Ain't nobody looking in yo face. If anything, I was looking to see what ignorant fool would be standing up on a couch."

"I see." Bone took another swig from his bottle. Without warning he turned the bottle upside down emptying the entire bottle of champagne on top of the woman's head. "How bout that?"

The woman quickly shot to her feet and lunged towards Bone, but before she could get to Bone a big bouncer roughly grabbed her in a choke hold and dragged her out of the club kicking and screaming.

On the way out of the club, Mike Murder cleared his throat and spit on the girl for good measures just to piss her off even further.

Bone took another swig from his bottle and shook his head. He had been in Miami for the past two weeks trying to gather as much info on Scarface as possible. He wanted to find out where his family lived and who his friends were so he could turn all of their lives upside down. The nerve of Scarface to send a woman to try and kill him. That alone pissed Bone off and what pissed him off even more was that Vicky had almost succeeded. Now it was his turn to cause havoc on Scarface's loved ones. He had put the word out on the streets that he was willing to pay anyone with some useful information on Scarface or his crew.

"Yo!" Mike Murder called out. "Shorty right here said she wanna holla at you."

Bone looked to see who Mike Murder was talking about. Standing next to Mike was a short dark skin chick who had on way too much make up. Her face wasn't anything to write home about, but the K. Michelle ass she had definitely grabbed Bone's attention. "Yeah send her over," he said still checking out the woman's assets. Her ass was so fat that he could see it from the front as she walked over towards him. "How can I do you? I mean what can I do for you?" Bone smiled and then turned his new bottle up to lips.

"Yeah I heard you had some bread for anyone who had any info on Scarface," she looking to read his facial expression.

"You got some info?"

"You got some bread?" the chick countered.

"Listen bitch" Bone said trying to keep calm. "If you got some info spit it out. If not, step the fuck off before I get upset."

"Dang," the girl said sucking her teeth. "You ain't gotta act like that I was just coming over here to tell you my homegirl got all the info you need. She was just afraid to come over here, so I just wanted to make sure you was the New York nigga that everyone was talking about."

"My bad love." Bone grabbed a hold of her hand and kissed it gently. "What's your name?"

"Tiff," she answered with a smile.

"And what's ya home girl's name?"

"Mya," Tiff replied.

"A'ight, why don't you go get Mya and tell her to come holla at me." Bone took another swig as he watched Tiff's ass switch and jiggle from side to side with each step she took. A minute later Tiff returned with a nice looking light skin woman with what looked like an expensive weave.

"This my friend Mya I was telling you about," Tiff said introducing the two.

"So ya friend here was telling me that you had some info that I might be interested in," Bone said taking a deep swig from his bottle.

"Yeah I know that bitch ass nigga Scarface," Mya said with venom dripping from her voice. "What you wanna know; where he live, where his mama live, where his businesses are located? What?"

Bone's lips spread into a smile. "I want to know everything, but can you give me a second. I would like to have a word with your friend for a second," he said looking over at Tiff. "Let me holla at you real quick."

Bone led Tiff out to the parking lot. His car was parked in the middle of the huge lot, but instead he took Tiff towards the back of the lot.

"Where we going?" Tiff asked with a goofy drunk look on her face.

"Right here," Bone said positioning her back up against a truck. His lips quickly found a home on the side of Tiff's neck.

"Mmmmm," Tiff moaned as her hand found Bone's belt and fumbled to unfasten it. Bone slipped one of Tiff big ass titties up out of her shirt and kissed and licked all over the perky brown nipple slowly. Her moans started off slow and then they became desperate.

Bone quickly spun Tiff around and made her place her hands flat on the hood of the truck. Then he hiked up her dress and slid her thong to the side. Bone took a second to put a condom on before slipping inside of Tiff's wet slice. He started off with slow powerful deep strokes just enough to get Tiff used to his size. Then he gripped both of her ass cheeks and spread them wide apart as he began to pound away pulverizing her insides.

"Oh my God!!! Fuck!!!" Tiff moaned and cursed and held on to whatever she could hold on to. Her orgasm came hard and fast in a series of waves. Her legs wobbled and she made sounds like she was drowning. Bone moved deeper inside her, held her waist, made her sit, tried to fill her up. "Take this shit off!" he demanded as he slapped Tiff's ass with force as he watched it jiggle. Bone slapped Tiff's ass again while he watched her remove the one piece mini dress from over her head. Besides the heels on her feet, Tiff now stood completely naked in the parking lot.

"Throw that shit back!" Bone said slapping her ass again but this time the other cheek. Tiff stood wide legged and pounded her ass violently back into Bone. Her ass smacking up against his torso sounded off loudly. Bone grabbed a handful of Tiff's hair and pulled her head back with a snap. He watched as her huge ass jiggled and bounced with each stroke he delivered.

"Ahhh, Yes! Yes!" Tiff moaned. Her eyes were closed tight and her mouth was wide open as she moved her head from side to side in pain and pleasure. She was sweating as if she'd just ran a marathon. Bone delivered five last strong strokes and then stiffened up and let out a loud groan. "Arghhhh!"

Bone removed the condom, picked Tiff's dress up off the ground and cleaned his dick off with it, then tossed the dress back down to the ground like it was a piece of trash, and then spun off leaving Tiff standing there looking stupid.

"Ass hole!" Tiff yelled at Bone's departed back as she picked her dress up off the ground and examined it.

Bone made his way back to the VIP section and popped open another bottle of champagne. He took a seat next to Mya. "Okay now where were we?"

"You wanted to know everything about Scarface. I hate his guts and want him dead so I'm pretty sure I can be of some help to you," Mya said with a devious I'm up to no good smile on her face.

"I think I like you already," Bone said returning Mya's smile.

13

BACK LIKE I NEVER LEFT

Six months later Capo was finally released from the box and allowed back into regular population. After unpacking all of his belongings inside of his new cell, Capo's next stop was the yard. It had been a while since he was allowed to walk around freely so this was something he would have to get used to again. Capo coolly bopped through the yard with his head held high. He knew that the entire jail had been talking about the action packed movie he had made in the gym six months ago. Capo enjoyed putting in work, but what he didn't enjoy was the sad look on Kim's face when she had visited him in the box.

Kim was a good woman and the last thing Capo wanted was to disappoint her or let her down. She had made him promise that once he was released from the box that he would stay out of trouble so that he wouldn't lose his good time and he would still be able to make it home early on good behavior. Capo agreed to stay out of trouble, but what Kim didn't understand was that in jail anything could happen and people fought and killed over the smallest things. He had made Kim a promise that he knew he couldn't keep. Kim would be mad, but hopefully she would forgive him.

Capo moved through the yard until he spotted Stacks and a few other Homies standing around talking shit to one another.

"What's good?" Capo asked giving everyone a pound.

"Looks like we got us a little problem on our hands," Stacks said and then nodded towards a bunch of mean looking men that stood in a group all wearing Kufis.

"Seems like ya man Cash done turned Muslim to keep us off his ass."

"Fuck him turning Muslim got to do with us?" Capo asked confused. He could care less what Cash had changed his religion to. When the two crossed each other paths again it was on and popping on site.

"Nah… You don't understand. The Muslims are the biggest gang in the jail system. You fuck with one of them and a riot is sure to pop off," Stacks explained. He knew the after math of fucking with the Muslims and he didn't think it was worth taking it to a further extent with them, especially if it wasn't over no money.

"Fuck that!" Capo spat. "And fuck them Muslim niggas... Shit done already went too far to stop now!" Capo could give two fucks about what organization Cash had joined. The fact still remained that lives had been lost and loved ones had been robbed and shot. It was already too turned up to turn down now. "What's up with that clown Wayne?"

"He's paying the Muslims for protection," Stacks told him.

"You can't be serious," Capo said in disbelief. "Niggas is stone cold gangsta's on the streets and then come to jail and turn Muslim. Un-fucking believable!" he raved. As Capo sat talking, he noticed Cash and Wayne both enter the yard at the same time. Just the sight of Cash made Capo's blood boil. Yeah he had put hands and feet on him, but that wasn't enough. He wanted Cash to bleed. He wanted him to see what real pain felt like and he definitely wanted him to know this shit wasn't a game by no means what so ever.

Cash and Wayne were immediately flanked by Muslims when they entered the yard. They stood over in a huddle talking in a hushed tone and every few seconds one of them would look back over his shoulder as if the organization was up to no good.

Capo didn't know what they were over there talking about, but if he had to guess more than likely it was about him.

"Here we go," Stacks said out loud as he noticed the gang of Muslims heading in their direction. Each man's face held a serious and dangerous no nonsense look on it. One of the Homies discreetly passed Capo a shank. When the two crews got within striking distance, the entire yard got quiet in anticipation of the violence that was sure to come next.

"Whats going on my brother?" a man wearing a colorful Kufis said. His voice was peaceful, but his eyes were the eyes of a killer. "I understand you have a problem with one of the brothers."

"You fucking right I have a problem with one of your brothers," Capo shot back. "And you or Allah won't be able to save him."

"Listen my brother," the Muslim said in a calm tone. "My name is Big Ock, and Cash is now a Muslim, so whatever problems you have or had with him in the past, I ask that you let it go and forgive him," he said. "And I can promise you that here on out you won't hear a peep out of him and you got my word on that. We come in peace."

Stacks quickly stepped in before Capo said something stupid and started an all-out war. "No problem, Big Ock. You keep him away from us and we'll stay away from him."

"I appreciate it my brother," Big Ock said with a head nod as him and his team of Muslims left and headed back over to the area of the yard that they just came from.

"Fuck is you doing?" Capo snapped once the Muslims were out of ear shot.

"Calm down," Stacks said. "I'm not starting an all-out war with the Muslims. If you want to make a move, then handle your business. Catch that clown Cash at another time. Just not right now. You just got out the box," he reminding Capo.

Capo wasn't trying to hear nothing that Stacks was talking about, but he had to admit that he was right. A war with the Muslim right now wouldn't benefit anyone. Not to mention there was nowhere for Cash to run since the two men were in the same jail together.

"Catch him alone on some one on one shit and handle your business," Stack said with a devilish smirk on his face.

Once the yard was shut down Capo headed back to his cell. He hadn't spoken to Kim in a while so he figured he'd sit down and write her a letter. Kim had written Capo plenty of letter, but the officers who worked the box area didn't like Capo so they held on to his mail. They even played games with his food some nights. Capo stepped in his cell and was pissed off immediately. All of his things had been removed from the bottom bunk and sloppily placed on the top bunk. His bunkie laid on the bottom bunk with his legs crossed at the ankles with a ButtMan magazine in one hand while his other hand was resting in his sweatpants.

"Yo fam what's good?" Capo asked standing over the man in the sweatpants.

"What's good my nigga," he replied as if nothing was wrong.

"Yo why you moved all my shit from off my bunk and put it up on the top bunk?" Capo asked getting in a good position so he could steal on his cell mate.

"Nah I got a bad back. I can't be climbing up on the top bunk every night. It's quiet for all that," he said as if that was the end of the discussion.

"Oh you got a bad back? Why didn't you just say that from the beginning Homie," Capo said. Without warning he grabbed the man by his ankle and violently yanked him off the bed. "Nigga you think I give a fuck about ya stupid ass back?" Capo growled as he stomped his cell mate's head into the concrete floor until he stopped moving. "I'm trying to write my shorty a letter and you wanna be in here talking crazy," Capo said out loud to no one in particular as he removed all the man's things off the bottom bunk down onto the floor and neatly replaced all of his things back on the bottom bunk. Capo was already pissed off due to the fact that he couldn't touch Cash and his bunkie's ignorance pushed him over the top.

Capo laid on his bunk and began to come up with a strategy on how he could get close to Cash while he was alone and not surrounded by a gang of Muslims.

14

WHAT'S WHAT

Angela pulled the stolen vehicle into the garage of one of the several properties that she owned. The place was a one level house that sat on an unpopular street. Angela cut the car off and looked in the back seat at a sleeping Ashley. She was glad that she was able to sleep at a time like this, especially with so much going on. This was a lot for Angela so she knew this had to be a lot for a child. Ashley had no other choice but to trust Angela especially now that both of her parents were dead. Angela really wanted nothing to do with the situation, but she just couldn't leave the helpless little girl out there for dead like that. She knew if she turned her back on the situation that Ashley wouldn't be alive for no longer than twenty-four hours at the most. Angela figured her life was already jacked up so she might as well try to help better Ashley's life.

"Time to wake up," she said giving Ashley's shoulder a light tap. Ashley sat up and looked around. "Where are we?" she said while yawning and stretching.

"We're safe," was Angela's only answer. They stepped foot inside the house through the garage and Ashley immediately noticed that an old looking sofa was the only piece of furniture that decorated the living room. The kitchen didn't look any better. Immediately Ashley knew she wasn't going to like the place. This wasn't a place built or set up for a child.

"What's wrong?" Angela asked sensing that something was wrong.

"This place looks creepy," she confessed. "I want to go home."

Angela squatted down in front of Ashley so the two could see eye to eye. "Listen Ashley you're never going to go home and those men will never stop trying to kill you unless you start being honest with me and tell me why everyone wants an innocent child dead. Did your father give you anything, or tell you anything before he died?"

Ashley paused for a second and then shook her head no. She hated lying to Angela but she was only trying to do the right thing. In the back of her mind she wanted all this madness to finally be over and done with.

"You hesitated!" Angela said in a stern tone. "Stop fucking around and tell me why everyone wants you dead!" she yelled in Ashley's face. She could tell that it was something that the little girl wasn't telling her.

Ashley said nothing.

"I can no longer help you," Angela said with a defeated look on her face. "If you're going to keep secrets, there's nothing else I can do for you. There's the front door," she bluffed.

Ashley's head hung low to the floor as she dug down in her pocket and removed the thumb drive that her father had given her. She held it out towards Angela. "My father told me not to show or give this to anybody," she said as pregnant tears dropped from her eyes. "I'm showing you this and giving it to you because I trust you."

Angela took the thumb drive from Ashley's hand and then pulled her in and hugged her tightly as the little girl cried on her shoulder. "It's going to be okay," she said rubbing Ashley's back in an attempt to calm her down.

"My mother is dead isn't she?" Ashley asked out the blue in between sobs.

Angela nodded her head yes as she found herself crying right along with little Ashley as the two hugged one another tightly. She could only imagine what the young child was going through, how she felt, or how scared she had to be right at this moment. To wake up one day and never see your parents ever again would be hard for any child to handle and honestly Ashley was handling the situation like a trooper. Deep down inside Angela was happy and proud that Ashley was beginning to trust her. "I promise I won't let anyone hurt you," Angela told her.

"They're not going to stop until they find me," Ashley said wiping her face dry with the back of her hand. A part of her felt like she would be killed any day now. While another part of her felt safe when she was with Angela.

"Let me worry about the bad guys," Angela said. "Besides this place is out in the middle of nowhere. I highly doubt anyone will find us here." She also knew she had set up several trip wires around the house so if anyone tried to creep up on them, she'd see them coming from a mile away.

Angela walked over to the freezer, opened it, and then yelled. "Who wants ice cream?"

Angela ordered pizza and did her best to make Ashley feel as comfortable as possible. No child deserved to die because of a mistake that their parents made. Angela knew that Ashley wasn't really her problem, but there was no way she could just leave the little girl for dead. Ashley's problems had now become her own problems. As Ashley sat down eating a slice of pizza, Angela took apart a 9mm and began to clean it and piece it back together. She wanted to make sure that if any trouble did show up that she'd be ready. Angela had no clue how this entire situation was going to play out, but she liked her chances.

"How did you learn how to kill so good?" Ashley asked helping herself to a seat on the sofa next to Angela with her eyes focused on the gun in Angela's hands.

Angela smiled. "It took years of practice and killing is very bad," she said making it crystal clear that there was nothing fun about killing someone.

"It looks fun like a video game," Ashley said returning Angela's smile.

"Trust me this ain't no video game," she said seriously. "Once you get shot, you don't get another life or another chance to complete the level. That's it when you're dead, you're just dead."

"Can you teach me everything you know?" Ashley asked.

Angela laughed, until she realized that Ashley was dead serious. "You're just a kid!" Immediately thoughts of her training James popped into her mind. She had remembered when James had asked her the same thing and because of her he was now dead.

"So you started when you were a kid right?"

"Yeah that was different," Angela said quickly. "I didn't want to become a killer. It was forced upon me."

"Just like it's being forced upon me right now," Ashley countered. It excited her to watch Angela kill with ease, move around, and barely get noticed as if she was invincible.

"You have your whole life ahead of you," Angela began. "You still have time to be anything you want to be." She refused to let Ashley throw her life away like she had done hers. If she could go back and change everything, she would change it in a heartbeat. No one wanted to kill and murder people for a living, and live life as if they didn't even exist.

"I want to be like you," Ashley replied. "The way you handle yourself, the way you're untouchable, and the way no one can touch you. I want to be just like you."

Angela shook her head as she thought about how to explain to her that there was a better way to live than what she did for a living. It may have seemed exciting, but with the job also came the bullshit. "Listen," she said. "I know you don't want to go on with life never being able to enjoy yourself. Don't you want to have some kids? Get married? Travel the world? Well if you do what I do, then the only one thing you may be able to do is travel the world, but then you still won't be able to enjoy it."

"I don't care!" Ashley shrugged.

"No," Angela replied. "Trust me you'll thank me later. Now go brush your teeth and get ready for bed" she said ending the conversation at that. She definitely understood how little Ashley felt, but there was no way that she was going to turn an innocent little child into a killer and ruin her life. She watched as Ashley stood in front of the mirror in the bathroom brushing her teeth with a sad look on her face.

"I ain't falling for the puppy eyes," Angela laughed to herself. Once Ashley was done in the bathroom Angela offered her the bedroom, but Ashley declined and chose to sleep on the floor next to Angela.

Ashley may have been young, but she wasn't a fool. If someone kicked the front door down and started shooting, she wanted to be as close to Angela as possible. She felt safe when around Angela and knew that she wouldn't let any harm come her way. They hadn't known one another for that long, but that was one thing that was already understood and no denying.

Once Angela was sure that Ashley was sleep she got up from the floor and grabbed her laptop and powered it on. She just had to find out what was on that thumb drive that had everyone trying to kill an innocent child. Once the computer booted up, Angela stuck the thumb drive in and tried to gain access, but was immediately denied. The thumb drive needed a password in order to open.

"Shit!" Angela cursed and snatched the thumb drive out of her laptop and stuck it down in her bra. For the rest of the night Angela would be raking her brain wondering what was on that thumb drive.

The next thing on Angela's objective was to find out who this detective that kept sticking his nose into business that didn't belong to him was. She pulled up the article about Detective Washington rescuing Ashley and got as much information as she could on him from the Internet. Angela didn't want to have to kill the detective, but figured him to be one of those super cops that wouldn't stop coming until his head was blown off. She read up on the detective for about another hour before lying down next to Ashley and going to sleep.

***

The next morning when Angela woke up, her eyes scanned the area first and then she quickly jumped up. She looked around the living room and Ashley was nowhere to be found. Panic quickly kicked in as she grabbed a knife from out of the kitchen then ran throughout the house in search of the child. Angela came to a halt when she reached the bedroom and saw little Ashley sitting on the bed fumbling around with a 9mm in her hand.

"What the hell are you doing!?" Angela snapped as she snatched the gun out of Ashley's hand. "Are you crazy? You could have killed yourself by accident!" she continued to rant. "This is not a toy!" she yelled holding the gun in the air. She was so pissed off with Ashley at that very moment. She had been going out of her way to protect this child and here she was putting herself in a situation where she could of easily killed herself by accident.

"Sorry," Ashley said in a voice below a whisper with her head hung low. "I was just trying to learn how to shoot," she said innocently.

Angela thought about continuing to scold Ashley, but then decided against it. Instead she leaned over and hugged Ashley tightly. "Sorry for raising my voice," she said. She knew how curious children could be and it was her fault for leaving a loaded firearm where a child could get a hold of it. She would have to start being more mindful, but the truth of the matter was this was her first time ever living with a child.

"It's okay. I shouldn't of had touched your gun while you were sleep," Ashley apologized. "I just figured you wouldn't let me see it if you were awake."

Angela paused for a second and then removed the clip from the gun and popped out the bullet that was in the chamber. "Here, let me show you how to hold it," she said with a smile. She knew that wasn't a smart thing to do, but seeing a smile on the little girl's face was priceless.

"Really!?" Ashley's face lit up like a Christmas tree. Angela stood behind Ashley and showed her how to hold the gun. For hours she showed Ashley how to hold and shoot the gun. After that was done Angela took Ashley out back and set up a few targets. She screwed a silencer on the barrel of the 9mm and handed the loaded weapon to Ashley.

"Okay breath," she instructed. "Take your time, visualize the target, make sure you're in tune with the target, and then pull the trigger."

Ashley stood there for a second. She was nervous and didn't want to mess up. Never in a million years would she have thought that she would be learning how to shoot a gun. She took a deep breath and then pulled the trigger knocking down the first target.

"Wow," Angela hummed. "Try the next target."

Ashley aimed the gun at the next target, paused, and then pulled the trigger. Again she hit the target.

Angela had never seen such a good shot at such a young age. "Ummm, are you sure you've never shot a gun before?" She asked in a joking tone of voice, but she was dead serious.

"Only on my video games and at the arcade," Ashley answered with an innocent smile. "Can I shoot some more?" She had only fired the gun twice and was already addicted. Her heart was pumping fast and her adrenaline was flowing.

"Sure," Angela said as she set up four more targets. The next round it only took Ashley six shots to hit four targets. Angela could tell that the more she practiced, the better her aim could get. It was already good so with a little practice and training, there was no telling how good Ashley could become.

"Looks like you're a natural at this," Angela said. For the rest of the night Angela set up target after target and showed Ashley the fundamentals of becoming an assassin. From shooting, to knife strikes, she even taught her a few take down moves that she could use if she was ever in a jam. Angela hated to admit it, but the more time she spent with Ashley the more she realized how much the little girl was just like her. At first she thought that Ashley was playing around when she asked her to train her, but the more Angela taught her, the more Ashley focused and paid close attention. After a few hours of training Ashley had the hand gun down pact. Ashley was knocking down targets left and right. She removed the empty clip and slapped a fresh clip in, in record time surprising herself and Angela all at the same time.

At the end of the night Ashley and Angela sat down on the floor with their legs folded up under them eating Chinese food enjoying a good laugh. Having someone else around wasn't turning out to be such a bad thing after all. Angela was definitely enjoying the company and she liked the fact that little Ashley looked up to her and wanted to be just like her. Yeah she knew what she did for a living was wrong and she by far was not a role model, but at the same time it felt good that someone thought so highly of her. It felt good to be around someone that didn't want or need anything from her, felt good to just be around some love for once. This was the closest Angela would ever come to being a mother and she couldn't deny that having Ashley around wasn't half bad. The more time she spent with Ashley, it made her wish that maybe she should have taken a different road in life; maybe she should have went out and got a regular job and lived like a normal person; got married and had a few kids.

"So what are we going to do if the bad guys come here trying to kill us?" Ashley asked shoving a fork full of rice in her mouth.

Angela smiled. "I'm going to kill them!"

"Can I help?"

"Absolutely not," Angela said quickly. "These men are professionals and you're just a child." There was no way she would allow Ashley to get involved in this mess. Teaching her how to shoot was one thing, but actually shooting someone was a whole other story.

"Two guns are better than one so I think you should let me help," Ashley said smiling. She knew Angela wouldn't allow her to actually kill someone, but it was worth a try.

"Nice try," Angela laughed. "Hopefully I won't have to kill anyone else."

15

AWAKING A
SLEEPING GIANT

Frank sat on the loveseat in his hotel room sipping on a glass of Cognac. In between his legs sat a young Brazilian prostitute. She had a soft pillow resting under her knees as her head bobbed up and down at a nice and slow rhythm. Frank sat in the loveseat and the only thing he could think about was his wife Kate. Images of her lying on the supermarket floor dead with a bullet in her head kept popping up in his head. The Teflon Queen had written a check that her ass wouldn't be able to cash. This was no longer business for Frank, it was now personal and he planned to personally watch Angela take her last breath. Loud slurping sounds snapped Frank out of his thoughts and forced him to look down at the beauty that was between his legs.

"You like that?" the prostitute said in a sexually charged voice. Then she turned her attention to Frank's balls, holding them in her hands and licking them assiduously like a cat while she looked up at him the entire time. Frank stood to his feet and began to thrust himself in and out of the prostitutes mouth at a fast pace. He grabbed two handfuls of her hair and began to fuck the prostitute's mouth like it was a pussy, like he wanted to choke her, like he was trying to fuck the life out of her. "Look at me!" he demanded and slapped the woman's face. The prostitute looked up at him with her eyes watery from gagging several times and saliva sliding out the corners of her mouth dripping from her chin down to her breast. She moaned loud and gagged even louder as she let Frank have his way with her mouth. With each stroke Frank delivered, he pictured himself stabbing Angela with a knife. He pictured himself punishing her for what she'd done. He pictured himself making her suffer for what she had done to Kate.

"That's it! Take it bitch!" Frank gasped, thrusting his pelvis harder and faster into the prostitute's mouth. Suddenly he pulled out and shot his load spraying cum all over her face. "Ahhhh yeah," he groaned as he shoved his dick back into the prostitute's mouth. "Suck it all out!"

The prostitute choked and gagged but managed to suck the rest of the cum out and swallow it like a good whore. She wiped her mouth with the back of her hand and then smiled up at Frank. "Was this mouth good to you?"

Frank smiled. "Yes it was amazing," he said as he peeled off a few hundred dollar bills and handed them to the Brazilian beauty.

The prostitute eyed the cash, smiled, and then looked up at Frank. "Damn! For this I can stay for the whole weekend if you like."

"Won't even be here for the whole weekend," Frank said standing up straight. "It was nice meeting you, but you have to go."

"Well the name is Spice, and I'll be twice as nice for the right price," she sang and handed Frank her card. "If you're ever back in town, give me a call honey." She kissed him on the cheek and then left.

Once Spice was gone, Frank took a quick shower and then prepared himself for what he knew would be a showdown. Mr. Clarke had called and informed him that Angela had attempted to gain access to the thumb drive. Once she tried to access the thumb drive, Mr. Clarke was able to trace the IP address to the computer and track down where the laptop was located that attempted to access the thumb drive.

Frank looked down at his phone and saw that Mr. Clarke was calling him. "Yeah," he answered.

"Tracked Angela down," Mr. Clarke said with his voice full of hope. "She's hiding out in a house in North Carolina. I want you and a few of my men to go out there and settle this once and for all. I need that thumb drive back," he said as if his life depended on it.

"Text me the address," Frank said in a cold tone. He was mentally and physically ready to go to war.

"I really need you to handle this once and for all. I either need that thumb drive or the little girl because she's the one that knows where it is."

"Not a problem text me the address," Frank said and then ended the call. At the moment he could care less about some stupid thumb drive. All that was on his mind was killing any and everybody affiliated with the so called Teflon Queen. Because of her, he had lost his best friend, because of her he had lost his lover, and most importantly because of her he had lost his soul mate, and for that reason alone Angela had to die. Frank packed a duffle bag with everything he would need and then headed out the door.

16

LITTLE ASHLEY

"Keep it steady and breath," Angela instructed in a light whisper as she lay next to Ashley. Ashley laid flat on her stomach in the middle of the woods. In her hand was a sniper rifle, and in her cross hair stood a deer. She took a deep breath and exhaled as she flipped the safety off and wrapped her finger around the trigger.

"Get in sync with the target," Angela whispered. Ashley stayed patient and when she felt the time was right she squeezed the trigger. Angela watched as the deer's head snapped to the side and then dropped down to the ground like a sack of rocks.

"You did good kid," Angela said like a proud mother.

"Can I do another one?" Ashley asked excitedly.

"No maybe tomorrow you already killed four deer today and six in the last two days," Angela pointed out. She hated to admit it, but Ashley was great for a beginner and with time and practice she was sure to become a beast and maybe even one of the best assassins to ever walk this earth. Angela still had second thoughts about training the young girl, but she seemed determined to learn and she was persistent about the craft. Angela knew it was wrong but she respected the fact that someone respected and loved the craft as much as Ashley did. She also had to teach Ashley to use her training for good instead of evil, because training in the wrong hands could get real ugly, real fast.

"Just one more please?" Ashley begged.

"Tomorrow," Angela said. "And hopefully we can find another deer. You may have killed them all" she chuckled.

"Aww man," Ashley whined as she quickly broke down the sniper rifle in a matter of seconds like an expert. Angela was amazed at how fast the young girl was able to learn as much as she had in such a short period of time.

"Let's get washed up and ready for dinner," Angela said as the two strolled through the woods headed back towards the house.

"What's for dinner?"

"I was thinking fried chicken and coconut rice," Angela answered.

"Can I help you cook?" Ashley asked with a smile on her face.

"Sure why not," Angela replied. Every time she looked at Ashley, she realized that she was all that the little girl had and she made it her responsibility to look after and protect her by any means necessary.

Once back in the house the two prepared dinner and sat down Indian style on the floor and enjoyed their food. They might not have had much but they were happy. Angela tried to go out and buy Ashley some toys and video games so she could play like a regular kid, but Ashley was anything but a regular kid. Other kids her age were into toys, cartoons, and pranks, but not Ashley. All she cared about was how to assemble and disassemble a rifle in one minute flat, and how it would feel to take a human life. She wondered if it would be as cool as it looked on TV. She was determined to experience what it felt like to take a human life. Ashley felt like the harder she trained and the more experience she had, she would be prepared when it came time to kill.

Once the two were done eating they both took turns polishing the other one's fingers and toes. Angela chose the color red and Ashley chose silver.

"I'm about to hop in the shower real quick. What are you going to get yourself into?" Angela asked as she stood up and stretched.

"I think I'll just play this," Ashley said holding up a video game. Angela grabbed the video game and read the title out loud. "Hit Man!" All she could do was shake her head. "Knock yourself out and I'll be back in a second."

"Wait before you go. Let's take a picture," Ashley said pulling out the camera that Angela had just brought for her. Usually Angela was against pictures. In her line of work something as simple as a picture could do a whole lot of damage, but tonight she figured why not. Angela placed her face up against Ashley's face and smiled as Ashley snapped the picture.

Ten minutes later Angela entered the bathroom and stripped down butt naked. She hurriedly stepped into the shower and let the water from the showerhead assault her face. The hot water felt good as it sprayed directly on her face. As Angela stood in the shower her hand found its way down to her clit. It had been so long since she'd been with a man. After dealing with James she called herself staying away from men period. Regardless of the fact, she still had needs and there was a strong fire building up between her thighs.

"Shit," she moaned as she flicked her fingers across her clit at a fast pace. Then she inserted two fingers inside of her slice while still using her thumb to massage her swollen clit. "Eeeww," she moaned louder. Her fingers moved as if they had a mind of their own or were possessed. Her breathing quickly went from regular to choppy as she felt her legs become weak. She hadn't realized how bad she needed this, how bad her orgasm cried to be released, how bad her body desired to be touched in all the right places. "Oh my God!!!" Angela's hand shot out and roughly grabbed the shower curtain as her orgasm erupted in a series of waves. Her fingers slowed down as her body finally came to a calm. "Damn," Angela laughed as she stepped out of the shower. She slipped on a matching black thong and bra set and slipped the thumb drive down into the front of her draws as she looked at the bruises that were on her face. They were clearing up nicely. She moved her wet hair from her face so she could get a better look at her face when her device started to go off signaling that someone had stepped through the trip wire that was set up all around the house. Then all of a sudden the lights in the entire house went out. "Shit!" Angela cursed as she grabbed her 9mm that rested on the edge of the sink and rushed out of the bathroom. As soon as she stepped foot out the bathroom, bullets started ripping through the house from each and every direction. Angela quickly dropped down to the floor and called out to Ashley. "Stay down!!!" she yelled as she army crawled over towards the stairs. Just as she got ready to slide down the stairs, the front door came busting open and several men ran in the house carrying assault rifles. The first two gunmen entered the house without a problem. The next man that tried to enter through the front door, Angela put a bullet through his head killing him on site. A few seconds passed as twelve men all came running through the front door all at once. Out of the twelve Angela was able to take three of them out immediately. Her eyes adjusted to the dark quickly as she eased her way down the steps. Angela didn't know how many men were inside of the house or how many more surrounded the house. She continued on down the stairs as the sound of Ashley screaming could be heard throughout the house.

***

When the lights went out Ashley instantly froze up. She wasn't sure what was going on or what was about to happen, but whatever was happening she knew it wasn't good. When the front door came crashing open, out of reflex Ashley screamed. She quickly shot up to her feet and grabbed a knife from off the counter and tried to make a run for it. She had only made it a few steps before a gunman roughly grabbed her by her shoulder.

Ashley quickly spun around and sliced the gunman's arm forcing him to release his grip. Ashley tried to escape towards the basement door but the gunman stuck his leg out and tripped her up. She hit the floor hard. The impact caused the knife to slip from her hand. She speedily hopped up and opened the basement door and flung herself down the steps before the gunman could get a hold of her. She rolled and tumbled over and over until she finally hit the floor. "Argh," she groaned as she struggled to lift herself up from off the floor. She looked up and saw four gunmen trotting down the stairs. Ashley quickly looked around for anything she could use as a weapon. Over to her left she spotted a shovel. She quickly crawled over towards the shovel. The first two men got it the worse. Ashley swung the shovel as if it were a baseball bat and hit the first gunman across the face. To her right a gunman tried to reach out and grab her, but Ashley quickly sidestepped his attempt and fired off a kick that landed between the man's legs sending him crumbling down to the floor. She drew back and went to take his head off with the shovel, but stopped when she felt the barrel of a gun being pressed to the back of her head.

"Move and I'll blow your head off!" the gunman barked.

***

Angela eased her way through the house when some movement coming from her left grabbed her attention. It was a man with a large caliber machine gun in his hand. She dropped to one knee as she raised her weapon and fired off a single shot. The bullet whipped the gunman's head back as it tore through his face. Angela quickly stepped over the body and searched for the next target. As she moved through the living room a figure crept up on her from behind and looped a string of wire around her neck and began trying to strangle the life out of her. The quick maneuver caused Angela to drop her gun as her fingers immediately tried to stop the wire from choking the life out of her. Angela quickly threw herself back, driving her attacker into the wall with a loud bang. Still her attacker held a tight grip on the wire. As the two fought and struggled crashing all throughout the living room Angela spotted the half empty wine bottle that sat on top of the counter. She reached out and grabbed the bottle by its neck and swung it back where his head would be. It connected with a satisfying "thunk"! She swung it again and this time feeling it break against his skull. Ignoring the pain from the wire around her neck, she stabbed behind her head with the jagged edge of the broken bottle, again, and again. Then she heard a muted exclamation as a warm gush of blood sprayed against her upper back. The grip on the wire loosened as

Angela bent forward flipping the dead man's body over her shoulder like a rag doll. Thick nasty blood covered her hair and face, but Angela paid the blood no mind as she quickly went to pick up her gun when another gunman appeared out of nowhere and almost walked right into her. The darkness was altering his vision. Once the gunman figured out what and who was in front of him, he tried to aim his gun at the target but her hand moved in a blur as she delivered an open palm blow to his nose breaking it on impact. The gunman reached for his nose with both hands dropping his machine gun. With the reflexes of a cat Angela caught the gun in mid-air and opened fire, sending several bullets into the gunman's stomach. She turned just in time to see movement coming from her right. Angela did an army roll and came up firing, painting the wall with the gunman's brains. Two more gunmen sprung from around the corner. Angela emptied the rest of her clip on the first gunman. The bullets riddled and rocked the man's body making it seem as if he was break dancing. The next gunman ran towards Angela and opened fire. A bullet grazed Angela's cheek as she jerked her head back just in a nick of time. The gunman fired off another shot just as his legs were swept from up under him. His head violently bounced off the floor and he quickly scrambled back up to his feet and threw a punch that missed Angela by a mile. Angela threw a quick jab that hit the gunman dead in his mouth. It wasn't a knockout blow, but it was a blow that filled his mouth with blood.

The gunman took a step back, reached down in his pocket, and extracted a switchblade. The blade snapped open and he lunged at Angela. She dodged the knife and kicked the gunman but he was ready for it. She felt the stiff muscles in his stomach tighten for the blow as he tossed Angela down to the floor. She quickly hopped back up to her feet and got ready to lunge towards the gunman when she felt something sharp stinging the bottom of both of her feet. She looked down and saw that the broken glass from when the gunmen had shot the windows out had cut up the bottom of her feet. Angela reached down and grabbed the string wire that the first gunman had tried to use on her. The gunman threw himself against her and she felt a stab of pain as the blade nicked her lower back even as she twisted to stay clear of it. She kneed the gunman and wrapped the wire around his neck. The muscles in Angela's arms bulged as she pulled against both ends of the wire until the man stopped moving. Angela grabbed her 9mm from off the floor and continued on throughout the house in search of little Ashley. For a second she felt like her heart would stop when she heard Ashley scream followed by the sound of three different guns being fired. All the noise seemed to be coming from down in the basement. Just as Angela reached the basement, the front door busted open and in walked Frank wearing all black, with a big assault rifle in his hand and a pair of night vision goggles covering his head and eyes. Angela disappeared around the corner as several bullets tore through the wall where her head was seconds ago.

Frank quickly went after Angela. He sprang around the corner ready to fire, but Angela wasn't there. He quickly looked around as he heard the back door slam shut. He ran at a fast pace to the door and snatched it open. Immediately he spotted a woman's figure in a green glowing light running out towards the woods. Without hesitation Frank opened fire swaying the gun back and forth taking out anything in its path. Frank flipped the switch on his M-203 turning his automatic rifle into a grenade launcher. He fired a grenade in the area he had last seen Angela. A big explosion erupted followed by several trees and tree branches falling. Frank quickly stuffed an oversize grenade in the gun and fired another grenade. The second explosion lit up the entire woods as well as set several trees on fire. Frank quickly scanned the woods area with his night vision goggles looking for any sign of movement. After scanning the woods for two minutes Frank figured Angela had to be dead and headed back to the house.

Frank stepped foot back in the house and yelled out to his soldiers to meet him out front. "Yeah no one would be able to survive two grenades," Frank said trying to convince himself that The Teflon Queen was in fact dead. What he really wanted was for Angela to stand her ground and fight him man to woman so he could look in her eyes as she took her last breath, but instead Angela had ran off and died like a coward.

Several seconds later several of Mr. Clarke's men exited the house with a little girl in their possession. Frank removed his goggles to get a good look at the girl to make sure they grabbed the right one.

"Angela is going to find me and kill you!" Ashley growled looking Frank in the eyes.

Frank laughed loudly as he turned and slapped the shit out of Ashley. "You stupid little fool! Angela is dead and you'll be joining her in just a few hours," he told her. "Now where's this thumb drive that I've been hearing so much about?"

Ashley looked at Frank and didn't say a word as if she didn't speak English. The one thing that she had learned from Angela was to keep her mouth shut. If she wanted to become an assassin, she knew she would have to start acting like one. Frank drew his hand back and slapped the shit out of Ashley again. "Oh you want to play tough? Well guess what?" he said not giving her a chance to answer. "I have ways of making little shits like you talk." Frank looked up at the soldiers that stood around. "Time to move!"

Mr. Clarke's men duct taped Ashley's wrist and feet together and placed a black pillow case over her head and tossed her in the back of a black van as if she was a piece of trash. Before Frank left, he turned and fired a grenade into the house before hopping in one of the van's as it peeled away from the house leaving the entire house in flames.

***

Angela rolled over and removed the tree branches and debris from her body as sat up and saw one side of her house go up in flames. "Shit!" she cursed when she thought about Ashley. She took all her strength and picked herself up off the ground and ran back towards the house. She hoped and prayed that Ashley was still alive but deep down inside she doubted that she was still alive. Angela entered the burning house and was glad to see that the fire hadn't really spread due to the fact that she didn't have much furniture. She started with the basement then worked her way up to her bedroom. Angela quickly grabbed a pair of jeans, a shirt, and several large stacks of money from the safe that sat in her closet and stuffed it down inside of her duffle bag. She then ran over to her gun closet and filled it with several different types of guns and plenty of ammunition. Once she had everything that she needed, she made a bee line for the back door and disappeared into the woods before the cops showed up.

A few miles down the road Angela found a low key looking motel and checked in. She needed time to sit down and come up with a plan to figure out what her next move was going to be. She figured if they hadn't killed Ashley that she would be safe as long as she had possession of the thumb drive. Angela had no clue what was on the thumb drive but whatever it was, it had to be very important or either worth millions. Angela opened a BC powered and took it dry to help with the pain and then hopped in the tub. Her body needed to soak in the hot water while she figured everything out.

Angela rested her head on the back of the tub as her mind wondered about how the gunmen had tracked them down. Inside she regretted leaving Ashley downstairs alone knowing how serious the situation at hand was. She should have kept Ashley by her side at all times no matter what. A million thoughts ran through Angela's mind as her body soaked in the steaming hot water. The first thing she had to figure out was how she was going to get Ashley back. From all of the events that had taken place it was safe to say that Ashley's life was on the clock. Angela knew she only had but so much time to find Ashley before her abductors killed her.

Angela stepped out of the tub and turned the TV on. She saw her face plastered all over the screen. Her picture sat in the right bottom corner of the screen with the words *"Armed And Dangerous"* written underneath. The reporter, reported about a gun fight that took place at the house Angela once called her own. Then a picture of Ashley popped up on the screen with the words *"Missing"* written underneath. Angela walked over and grabbed her duffle bag and sat it down on the bed. The first thing she pulled out was her twin .380's. She screwed a silencer on both of the barrels. All the fun and games were over. If they were trying to piss Angela off, they had succeeded and some blood was definitely about to get spilled.

17

FOLLOW THE BREAD CRUMBS

Detective Washington stepped pass the yellow tape and entered the house where Ashley was last seen. On the outside the detective was cool, calm, and collect, but on the inside he was furious. He didn't know who the man in the suit was from the supermarket, but he planned on tracking him down and taking him out by any means necessary. The way he had opened fire and killed so many innocent people in the supermarket flat out disgusted Detective Washington. After doing his research on the dead Japanese woman, Detective Washington found out that her name was Kate Chambers. She was wanted in several different states and had been on the FBI's most wanted list for a few years. She was married to a man named Frank Chambers.

When Detective Washington pulled up a picture of Frank, it was a perfect match of the same mad man from the supermarket. A picture of Frank was sent to every police and law enforcement station in the state. Now all Detective Washington had to do was be patience. He knew that killers like Frank could only stay quiet but for so long and once he made another peep, Detective Washington planned to nail him.

"Hey detective, come check this out," a uniform officer called out. Detective Washington walked over and squatted down as the officer handed him a little girl's shoe.

"Ashley was here," the officer said. "I just hope she's still alive." He handed the detective a zip lock bag full of different shell casings.

Detective Washington looked at all the empty shell casings and looked around at all the dead bodies that lay around the property. Something wasn't adding up. It felt as if something was missing from the scene. He just couldn't pin point what it was. He needed some answers. Detective Washington looked around at all the blood that was splattered on the walls and could only imagine what had taken place in this house. After giving the house a thorough search, several guns as well as plenty of ammunition was found along with a few passports and fake ID's; nothing useful just things that turned into more questions.

Detective Washington stepped outside the house, hopped back in his car, and pounded on the steering wheel. "Fuck!" he cursed loudly. After all the work he'd been doing, he still found himself empty handed and he still had no clue where Ashley could be. He didn't even know if she was dead or alive. In his eyes, this was all his fault because he had Ashley in his custody and let her get away. Detective Washington knew that the clock was ticking. He knew the longer Ashley stayed out there, the bigger the risk it was of her getting killed. Detective Washington pulled off in search of a liquor store. At a time like this, what he needed was a strong drink. For some strange reason whenever he had a drink, it helped his mind think clearer. As Detective Washington cruised down the street looking for a liquor store, he spotted a quiet low budget looking motel. Something in his gut was telling him to go check the motel. *"Fuck it,"* Detective Washington thought as he stomped down on the brakes and hit a U-turn. Detective Washington pulled into the parking lot and killed the engine. He stepped out the car and entered the door to the front desk of the motel. Behind the desk sat a filthy looking man dressed in a dingy wife beater and a pair of blue jeans. He was sleeping with his feet propped up on the desk. The smell of alcohol filled the air. Detective Washington noticed the man's face was rather dirty and it was covered in a rugged rough looking beard.

"Excuse me!" Detective Washington barked awaking the man who sat behind the desk out of his sleep.

"Yes how can I help you?" the man said wiping the corner of his mouth with the back of his hand as he leaned to the side and enjoyed a good stretch.

"I'm looking for this woman. Have you seen her?" Detective Washington asked holding up a photo of Angela.

"It depends," the man said rubbing his fingers together with a greedy look on his face.

Detective Washington reached down in his pocket like he was about to pull out some money, but instead he pulled out a gun and shoved it in the man's face. "Last time I'm going to ask you! Have you seen this woman!?"

"Ye.., ye.., yes she's in room 42 take it easy," the man said raising his hands in surrender.

"You got a key?"

"Yes, here!" the man said and then handed Detective Washington the key to room 42. "Just don't kill me."

Detective Washington left the front desk and headed straight to room 42. As Detective Washington eased his way towards room 42, he could feel butterflies in his stomach. The hairs on the back of his neck stood up and his palms began to sweat. The moment he had been waiting for was finally here. On a silent count of three, Detective Washington stuck his key in the lock, opened the door, and barged inside with his gun aimed forward. He stepped inside the room and to the naked eye the room appeared to be empty, but over pass the bed Detective Washington saw that the bathroom door was closed and he could see the light escaping from underneath the door. "Here we go," he said to himself as he reached the bathroom door. Just as he got ready to enter the bathroom he felt the barrel of a gun being pressed into the back of his head. *"Fuck!"* he whispered.

"Drop your weapon," Angela said in a stern voice.

"Listen to me! You don't want to do this! Killing a cop is not what you want to do," Detective Washington said standing frozen like a deer caught in the headlights. "Why don't we talk about this?"

"Please don't confuse me with a woman that likes to repeat herself."

With that being said Detective Washington slowly placed his gun down on the floor. "You're never going to get away with this."

"Your back up gun, where is it?" Angela asked.

"I don't have a backup," Detective Washington said as Angela gave him a quick pat down. Angela picked up Detective Washington's gun from off the floor. "So how did you find me?"

"A hunch."

Angela chuckled as she sat down in a chair that was stationed near the door. "Yeah some hunch."

"Where's Ashley?"

"They took her," Angela said as tears began to fall from her eyes. Deep down inside she had grown to love Ashley and she felt like she had let her down by letting her get captured. "You have to help me get her back."

Detective Washington slowly turned around with his hands still in the air as he walked over and sat on the edge of the bed. For some strange reason he felt safe and not like he was in the presence of a dangerous assassin. "How did you get involved in this? Did you kidnap that little girl?"

"No," Angela said shaking her head. "I was out minding my business and she ran into me. All of these men were after her. They were trying to kill her and I was just simply trying to protect her."

"I believe you," Detective Washington said as he inched his way over towards Angela and embraced her. He gave her a tight hug and tenderly rubbed her back. "Thank you for trying to help the little girl out. She spoke very highly of you when I was questioning her."

"I have to get her back," Angela sobbed.

"We'll figure something out," Detective Washington said. He had no clue what he was going to do, but he knew he would have to do something and do it fast.

"I need to know everything on a man named Mr. Clarke."

Detective Washington chuckled. "There's probably a million Mr. Clarke's out there. I'm going to need more information on this guy."

"Look for the Mr. Clarke who has the most money because the Mr. Clarke that's funding this has money out the ass," Angela told him. She knew it had to cost a grip to produce man after man to come after a child and not to mention the two hired guns.

"I think I can do that," Detective Washington smiled. "And what are you going to do once you have all of this information?"

"I'm going to put a bullet in his fucking head!"

"No," Detective Washington snapped. "You can't put a bullet in his head. I want to slap the cuffs on this Mr. Clarke guy!"

"Deal," Angela said as the two shook on it. A loud commotion led Angela and Detective Washington over towards the window. Detective Washington peeked out the window and saw the filthy man who worked at the front desk leading a pack of police officers towards the room.

Angela immediately grabbed her twin .380's and prepared to do battle.

"No let me handle this," Detective Washington said as he pulled a business card out of his pocket and handed it Angela. "I'll find out what I can about this Mr. Clarke guy and you stay out of trouble and keep in contact with me. I want to hear from you at least once a day."

"You got it," Angela replied as she watched Detective Washington disappear out the motel room door. Still not sure if she could trust him Angela kept her gun in her hand as she peeked through the blinds.

***

Detective Washington stepped out the room and flashed his badge. "Detective Washington," he introduced himself. "What seems to be the problem?"

"Yeah that's him right there! Arrest that man! He pulled a gun on me!" the filthy looking man said pointing at Detective Washington.

Detective Washington quickly pulled out the photo of Angela and explained to the officers that he was in search of the armed and dangerous woman that's been on everyone's TV. He then quickly led the officers away from room 42. He too wasn't sure if he could trust Angela, but he knew it was the only way he'd be able to find the girl and the crazed killer that called himself Frank. Plus after finally seeing and speaking to Angela in person, he left the motel room with a good vibe. He could tell that she genuinely loved little Ashley and that she would risk her own life to protect the child. If Mr. Clarke was the piece that would connect all the missing links then he planned on getting started on him today.

***

Angela peeked through the blinds and breathed a sigh of relief when she saw Detective Washington leading the other officers away from the room she stood in. She was prepared to kill each and every one of those officers if she had to. Angela walked over and flopped down on the bed. She had to come up with a plan before it was too late. She knew the longer Ashley remained missing, the higher the chance of her being killed was. First things first, Angela knew she had to relocate to another motel just in case Detective Washington turned out to be a snake.

18

WHAT NOW

Ever since Scarface was released from jail, Shekia had noticed a change in him, not a bad change but a change for the better. He was now trying more, trying to do the little things that he used to ignore and Shekia loved it. It was as if he left a boy and had returned a man. Yes it may have only been a few weeks but none the less she was thankful. Shekia stood in the kitchen fixing breakfast wondering when would be a good time for her to tell Scarface that she was pregnant. While Scarface was away, the thought of getting rid of the baby crossed Shekia's mind a few times. Not because she didn't want the baby but because she didn't want to raise a child without a father. But now things were different. Scarface was home and acting like a brand new man and doing everything in his power to not only make, but to keep Shekia happy. The only thing that bothered Shekia was the 'what ifs'. What if Scarface wind up having to do time in the long run? What if he wind up going back to his old ways, and what if this new him was only a faze.

"Hey baby," Scarface said. His voice startled Shekia causing her to jump. "My bad."

"Hey sorry you scared me," Shekia said holding her chest for extra emphasis. "You hungry?" she asked as her eyes went down to the butt of the gun that rested in Scarface's waistband. "What's the gun for?"

With that one question Scarface could see Shekia's whole attitude shift in a negative direction. "What do you mean what's the gun for? I've always carried a gun."

"Yeah, but you told me you weren't going to be living like that anymore."

"Living like what? I'm in the house," Scarface said with a confused look on his face. He didn't have the heart to tell her that Bone was in town and it wasn't no telling what would happen if or when the two crossed paths. One thing Scarface knew was that he wasn't about to get caught slipping.

"Nevermind! Just forget it!" Shekia snapped as she started slamming things around in the kitchen.

"Just forget what?" Scarface asked confused.

"Just forget everything!"

"You don't mean that?"

"Hmmp! Yes I do! Shit, for all I know you probably still fucking that whore Mya!" Shekia knew that was a low blow, but at the moment she could care less. The truth was she just couldn't get over him dealing with Mya and going over to her house without her knowing about it.

"I thought we were past that," Scarface said rubbing the bridge of his nose.

"Well you thought wrong!"

"What are you so mad about," Scarface asked. "I mean I just don't get it. I'm trying to do everything the right way now and it's like that's still not good enough for you."

"I think it's best if I go," Shekia said. She tried to walk pass Scarface but his arm shot out and grabbed her arm stopping her momentum.

"Fuck you mean it's best if you go?" Scarface snapped. "So as soon as shit don't go your way you just wanna leave right?"

"Scarface let's not play these games. It is obvious that you care more about the streets than you do me. Your sister getting killed ain't teach you nothing?" Shekia snapped and then walked off.

"What the fuck you just said!?" Scarface barked as he went after Shekia. He roughly grabbed her and spun her around so she could face him. He raised his hand to hit her when bullets came flying through the front door and windows. "Get down!" Scarface yelled as he tackled Shekia down to the floor and covered her body with his own. He pulled his pistol from his waist and clutched it tightly. As soon as the gunfire ended, Scarface hopped back up to his feet and ran out the front door hoping to find any of the gunmen, but instead all he saw was a minivan turn the corner in a hurry.

"Fuck!" he cursed loudly. He knew this had to be the work of Bone and his crew. He wondered how they got the scoop on where he rested his head especially since not many people knew where he lived to begin with. Scarface walked back inside the house and saw Shekia laying on the floor with a scared look on her face crying. "You alright baby?"

"I can't live like this no more!" Shekia screamed and ran upstairs.

Scarface called Black and told him to come over as soon as he could with a few soldiers as he heard loud movement coming from upstairs. Scarface ran upstairs and saw Shekia crying piling clothes into a suitcase.

"So that's it?" he asked plopping down on the bed.

"I can't live like this no more Scarface!" Shekia yelled. "When are you going to grow up!?"

"You talking like I shot my own house up!" Scarface snapped. "I've tried to change my whole life around. This is my past coming back to haunt me."

"Yeah well I'm not sticking around to get hit by a stray bullet. Fuck that! I have better things to do with my life."

"Like what?" he asked. The longer Scarface stood in the room with Shekia the angrier he was becoming. Not wanting to make matters worse, he decided to go downstairs and just let Shekia leave. He knew there was no use sitting around fighting with her. If she wanted to leave then she must not have really loved him to begin with.

Scarface made it back downstairs just as Black and three other men dressed in dark color clothing entered the house.

"What happened?" Black asked showing that he was ready to put in work at the drop of a hat.

"Bone made the first move," Scarface said pouring himself a drink. "I need y'all to find out where this motherfucker is hanging out at." Bone had officially crossed the point of no return. First he killed Vicky and now he had shot Scarface's house up. Enough was enough and it was time for Bone to die.

"I been pounding the streets to see what kind of info I could get on him and some stripper chick I used to mess with told me that him and his crew have been going to the club that she works at every other night." Black paused. "It's kind of like he wants us to be able to find him."

"They say motherfuckers should be careful about what they ask for," Scarface growled. Black got ready to reply, but paused when he saw Shekia dragging two suitcases down the stairs.

"You sure you don't wanna talk about this baby?" Scarface called out. Shekia stuck up her middle finger and exited the house, never breaking her stride.

"Maybe you should go after her," Black suggested.

Scarface waved him off. "Let that bitch go!" He was too through with Shekia and he was tired of her trying to leave every time something didn't go her way. Right now he had bigger things to worry about and he didn't have time to go running behind Shekia.

Scarface turned and faced Black. "You know where this strip club is?"

Black nodded his head with a devilish grin on his face. "Sho do!"

"Strap up. It's time to show this clown how we do things out here in Miami," Scarface said.

***

Three vans filled with killers holding automatic weapons pulled into the parking lot of the strip club. Each man in the van was ready to kill at Scarface's command.

"What's the plan?" Black asked.

"Simple, the bouncers not going to let us in the club with all these guns so we gon go in there and start an altercation and bring the party outside." Scarface turned and faced Knuckles. Knuckles was a beast who had just gotten out of prison and he was ready to prove himself in any way necessary. His muscles were so big that it looked as if the thread in his black thermal shirt was going to rip at any given moment. "Can you handle that?"

Knuckles looked at Scarface like he had just insulted him. "Of course I can handle that!" Knuckles had spent most of his life in and out of jail and was all for being violent and using extreme force in even the smallest situations.

"A'ight good! I'm going to send Youngin in there with you," Scarface told him. Youngin was a young knuckle head that always found himself in the middle of some drama. "I just got word that Bone and his team are in there. Y'all go in there and slap that nigga Bone around a little bit. All I need y'all to do is bring this clown outside and we'll take it from there."

"Say nomore," Knuckles said as him and Youngin hopped out the van. "This won't even take five minutes," Knuckles said cockily as him and Youngin disappeared inside the strip club.

"You think those two can handle this?" Black asked with a raised brow.

"We about to find out," was Scarface's only response.

19

'BOUT THAT LIFE

Bone sat on the couch as a thick chocolate stripper gyrated sexily on his lap. He sprinkled a few singles on her back as he took a deep swig from his bottle. Juicy J's new song blasted through the speakers at a high level. The base from the speakers had the strippers losing their minds.

Bone sat back watching the stripper do her thing, and the only thing that was on his mind was how he was going to slide off with one of these sexy dancers. Bone and his crew had only been in Miami for a few weeks, but to him it felt like a few months. He had already set up his operation and flooded a few well known spots with dope. He also had a few strippers moving E pills as well as a few pain pills right out of the strip club. He planned on turning the city upside down with his shenanigans. Bone looked around and smiled as he watched his crew. It seemed like they were having the time of their lives and Bone was loving every minute of it.

"I get off in a few hours," the stripper who resided on Bone's lap purred. "You'd tryna play or what?"

Bone looked down at her ass before he replied. "I'll think about it," he said in a cocky manner. The stripper on his lap had a fat ass, but it wasn't the fattest ass in the club and Bone wasn't the type to settle. He quickly shoo'd the girl off his lap and popped open a fresh bottle and took a swig. While the champagne set in, Bone's mind started to think about Mya. The information that she had given him paid off dearly when him and a couple of shooters drove by and shot up Scarface's house. Bone could have done more, but he didn't want to risk too much especially since he wasn't sure if anyone was home or not. The shooting was just the beginning. He had a whole lot more lined up and waiting for Scarface. Bone took another swig from his bottle as Mike Murder walked up and stood next to him. "What's good my nigga? You enjoying yourself?"

"Yeah, I was enjoying myself until I spotted those two clowns over there watching you like a hawk," Mike Murder said discreetly nodding in the direction of the two guys.

Bone lifted the bottle to his lips and glanced over at the two men. "Look like two bozo's to me," he shrugged. "How you think we should play it?"

"I'mma go over there and pop that bottle" (swing on him) Mike Murder said.

"Fuck it! You know I'm always down for some ignorant shit," Bone said smiling. Mike Murder walked over and informed three of his shooters to go outside and get the hammers from the car and wait for them to come out the club. He wanted to make sure that they were all protected.

"It's show time," Bone said smiling while he watched the two men make their way over towards where they stood.

***

"Look at these fools laughing and throwing money around like they own the whole fucking world," Knuckles complained. He hated when guys from out of town came into his town and tried to act like it was their town. It really pissed him off.

"These fools don't look so tough to me," Youngin said leaning up against the wall with his arms folded across his chest like he was posing for a magazine. All Knuckled and Youngin wanted to do was impress Scarface so they could move up in the ranks and start making some real money. Tonight would be the night that they earned their wings, but in order to earn their wings they would have to complete the mission that lied ahead.

"Man fuck all this waiting around shit. Let's go handle these niggaz," Knuckles said as he started walking in Bone's direction. Knuckles wasn't the type to just sit around and wait for shit to happen. He was the type to go out and make things happen. Knuckles and Youngin tried to walk up on Bone but was stopped by a few of his goons.

"You lost or something nigga?" a slim frame man with a thick nappy beard spat stepping in Knuckle's path.

"I need to have a word with ya man Bone," Knuckles demanded. From his body language one could tell that trouble was sure to follow.

"Fuck is you?" Bone said stepping to the front line with a smirk on his face. He lived for shit like this and couldn't wait to see how this would play out.

"Listen I'mma tell you straight like this," Knuckles began. "This my city and don't shit go on in this city without me being involved."

Bone and Mike Murder laughed loudly right in Knuckles face as if he wasn't standing right there. "Nigga you must got me fucked up," Bone said as one of his goons busted Youngin over the head with a champagne bottle knocking him unconscious on impact. Before Knuckles knew what was going on, Bone had already stole on him. The punch had stunned Knuckles and sent him stumbling backwards but he still managed to keep his footing. Bone's goons attacked Knuckles like a pack of wolves. The punches rocked Knuckles back and forth. Once he cleared the cob webs out of his head, Knuckles went crazy. Knuckles strike was so swift that even the people watching barely saw him swing. The goon that got caught with the punch rocked once on his heels before falling face first to the floor. Knuckles turned to the next man and grabbed him and tossed him across the room like a rag doll.

Bone flicked open a small pocket knife and jabbed it in Knuckles stomach and chest area several times while his goons went to work on the big man. Just as Knuckles got a second wind, Mike Murder hit him over the head with a chair on some wrestling shit dropping the big man down to his knees.

Bone quickly rushed over to where Youngin laid unconscious and hopped up on a couch and jumped off stomping down on Youngin's head. Before things could get further out of hand, several bouncers ran and broke up the violent scuffle. Once the fight was broken up the bouncers forced Bone and his crew out of the club.

Bone stepped foot outside and immediately something didn't feel right. Before he got a chance to put Mike Murder on to what he was feeling, shots started ringing out.

"Shit!" Bone cursed as he quickly dashed back inside the club as bullets whizzed by his head.

Out in the parking lot Scarface and his team opened fire as soon as they spotted Bone and his team exit the club. Scarface held down on the trigger of his gun until he ran out of bullets. The old Scarface would have reloaded and kept firing but the new Scarface was fresh out on bail facing murder and kidnapping charges so he decided to fall back. "Come on, we out!" Scarface ordered until a few of Bone's goons began to return fire. Scarface and his team quickly burned rubber and fled the scene before the police showed up.

Once the gunfire ended, Bone stood and examined the damage. Several of his goons laid stretched out dead. Blood was everywhere and so were several dead bouncers as well as dead innocent club goers. Loud sirens snapped Bone out of his thoughts.

"Come on bro we gotta go!" Mike Murder said in an urgent tone.

"Scarface," Bone said out loud. "It was Scarface and his peoples," he said as if he had just figured out a puzzle.

"We'll handle him later, but right now we have to go!" Mike Murder said rushing Bone in the back seat of the truck. Just as the cops showed up Mike Murder pulled out of the parking lot speeding.

20

CAKE AND ICE CREAM

Capo lay on his bunk reading a book. He had been doing a lot of reading over the past few months. Trying to come up with a way to get back at Cash was becoming too stressful. The Muslims were too deep in the jail system and it seemed like you could never catch one of them alone or by themselves. So instead of stressing himself out Capo began to start reading. He needed to find something to get his mind from a negative place to a positive one and books did just that for him. Just as Capo's mood seemed to be getting better, his mood quickly darkened when a loud fart sounded off. He took a sniff and something smelled as if someone or something had died. Capo quickly hopped up off his bed and looked up at his bunkie who lay on his bed with a pair of head phones covering his ears. Ever since their altercation over the top and bottom bunk, the two men hadn't said one word to the other until today.

"Damn nigga! Did you just shit on yourself?" Capo asked with his face crumbled up. The smell was so bad that he wanted to kick the man's ass again.

"My bad my shit been bubbling all day," the man said rubbing his stomach.

"Well next time you need to hold that shit in or something." And just like that Capo's entire day had been ruined. It didn't take much to piss him off especially since he was already mad for most of the day anyway. Being incarcerated was beginning to suck the life out of him. There were days when he just wished he could be home sitting in his hot tub sipping on a glass of vodka with a bad bitch between his legs. Every time he looked at his Bunkie, violent thoughts came to his mind and he felt a twitch in his hand.

"Yo listen next time you need to hold that shit until it's time to go to programs or chow or something," Capo spat with an attitude. "Got the whole cell smelling like shit!" he continued to rant. The more he thought about it and the longer he had to smell the foul odor the more he wanted to snuff his bunkie.

"A'ight fam I got you," the bunkie said just to shut Capo up. He was tired of Capo's cocky attitude and he didn't appreciate the way he spoke to or treated him. He kept quiet because he didn't want no problems with the bloods, but Capo was beginning to violate telling him he couldn't fart. Next he would be telling him that he couldn't speak. Capo's bunkie planned on getting a shank from one of his homeboys when he went out to the yard today, so the next time Capo said some fly shit out of his mouth he planned to stab his cocky disrespectful bunkie.

"And clean this place up while I'm gone too," Capo said as he threw on a crisp Polo shirt and began to brush his waves. Today one of his shorty's was coming to visit. A chick he used to mess with named Sabrina. Sabrina was a super freak. Capo called her and told her to come see him in hopes that she would be able to lift his spirits. A C.O. came and cracked Capo's cell and escorted him down to the visiting room.

Capo stepped foot in the visiting room and instantly a smile spread across his face when he spotted Sabrina sitting at the table looking as thick and sexy as ever. She wore a tight fitting long red dress that came down to her calves.

"Damn," Capo said as he hugged Sabrina tightly and inhaled her perfume.

"Oh my God it seems like I haven't seen you in forever," Sabrina said in a bubbly tone. "I know you better grab this ass," she growled in his ear. Capo gripped both of Sabrina's ass cheeks and gave them a squeeze which got him a few distasteful looks from the C.O.'s that worked in the visiting room.

"So how have you been?" Sabrina asked. For some reason she just couldn't stop smiling.

"I'm better now that you're here with ya fine ass," Capo said as he leaned across the table and kissed Sabrina on the lips.

"And I did just like you said and didn't wear no panties," she said with a devilish smile on her face.

"Oh really?" Capo said returning her smile. He hadn't seen Sabrina in a while but out the blue decided to call her up and see how she was doing. Sabrina had always been a rider and she had always loved Capo.

"I left two hundred on your books."

"You ain't have to do that baby. I'm good on the money tip," Capo said quickly. "I should be asking you do you need any money."

"Nah I been straight," Sabrina said smiling. "You know ya girl stay on the grind."

"Word? What you been getting into lately?" Capo asked nosily.

"I've been doing pick-ups and drop offs for Livewire," Sabrina whispered. "You know Livewire right?"

"Not personally, but I've heard of him" Capo said. "You be careful dealing with him. I heard him and his crew been beefing heavy with that Pauleena chick."

"Yeah I stay out of that mess. I get my money and that's it," Sabrina told him.

"I missed you," Capo said as he snuck his hand under the table and rubbed his fingers across her clit and smiled when his fingers became moist. "Oh it looks like somebody else missed me too," he said as he began to move his fingers around in a circular motion. Greedy sounds came from Sabrina as she spread her legs open even wider. "You missed this pussy? Huh?"

Capo didn't respond. Instead he slipped two fingers inside of her while his thumb rested on her swollen clit causing Sabrina's legs and breathing to get tense. Sabrina began to slowly gyrate her hips on Capo's fingers while making curt sounds like mmm and ahhh before she came violently. Her orgasm caused her moans to rise.

Capo quickly kissed her. He did that to shut her up. He began to move his fingers even faster while biting down on Sabrina's bottom lip.

"No stop bab… Baby I can't take it," Sabrina begged.

Capo ignored her cries and began to work his fingers even faster.

21

SURPRISE

SURPRISE

Kim pulled into the jails parking lot and killed the engine. After to speaking to Capo on the phone she could tell that him being locked up was really beginning to kill his spirit and hearing him sound like that was eating her up on the inside. So she decided to surprise him with a visit. She was sure that seeing her face would surely brighten up his mood and lift his spirits. Kim had been doing the best she could to make ends meet while Capo was away. The money wasn't coming in like it was before Capo got arrested, but no matter what she still held it down and never complained. Kim walked through the first metal detector before a female C.O. scanned her front to back with a hand held metal detector. The female officer chuckled as she looked Kim up and down. "Enjoy your visit," she said in a sarcastic tone.

Kim brushed the female officer off as a hater. The only thing on her mind was lifting the spirits of Capo. She knew Capo liked to get freaky during their visits so she wore a tight fitting sun dress that came down below her knees so that she wouldn't have any problems out of the officers and as usual she didn't wear any panties. "Hi you doing today Rick," Kim spoke to one of the regular visiting room officers. She had been up to see Capo so much that most of the officers knew her by name and vice verses.

"Ummm hey," Officer Rick said in a funny tone. "Table 26" he said with his head down.

Kim walked through the visiting room with her head held high. Her heels clicked and clacked loudly on the floor. Kim's smile quickly turned upside down when she saw Capo already sitting down at table 26 kissing another woman. Kim quickly walked over and joined the two at the table.

"So this what the fuck you do when I'm not around?" Kim growled catching Capo and his little girl friend off guard.

Capo looked at Kim and thought he was seeing a ghost. The last person he ever expected to see was Kim. "Ummm baby what you doing here?" he stuttered quickly lifting his hands from under the table.

"Ain't you going to lick your fingers?" Kim asked snaking her neck. "That's what you always do when you finish playing with my pussy, go ahead and lick your fingers I dare you."

"Damn bitch you could of at least let a bitch get her shit off first before you came raining on our parade," Sabrina said sucking her teeth. "You dusty bitches kill me!"

Capo stood up in an attempt to stop the inevitable but he was too late. Kim's hand shot out in a blur as she slapped Sabrina across her face twice before she even knew what hit her.

"Bitch!" Kim barked as she grabbed a hand full of Sabrina's hair and threw several blows with bad intentions. "You up here sneaking around...with my man...and you wanna...talk some tough shit!" Kim yelled with every blow she threw until several C.O.'s rushed over and separated the two women.

Several minutes later the lieutenant came over towards Capo's table. "Listen scum bag," was how he began the conversation. "Two options, one you can go back to your cell or two you can keep one of your visitors and send the other one home."

"I'll choose option number two," Capo said quickly.

"Who's staying and who's going?" the lieutenant asked in a stank nasty tone.

"I would like for Kimberly to stay," Capo told the lieutenant.

"Next time some bullshit like this happens I'm going to terminate all of your visitation rights for ninety days," the lieutenant said and then walked off.

"Shut the fuck up," Capo mumbled once the lieutenant was out of ear shot. He couldn't stand how the officers acted. It was crazy what a little bit of power could do to a person. Capo quickly dismissed the stupid lieutenant from his mind as he began to formulate a plan on what he was going to say to Kim when they allowed her back inside the visiting room. He knew Kim was a loyal chick and the last thing he wanted to do was hurt her or make her look or feel stupid. Capo had a lot of love for Kim and didn't want to mess up the relationship that the two shared.

Ten minutes later Kim was allowed back into the visiting room. She walked slowly towards table 26 with an embarrassed look on her face. With every step she took, she could feel everyone in the visiting room eyes on her. Kim sat down across from Capo and stared a hole through him. If looks could kill Capo would have been dead five times by now.

"Baby I can explain," Capo began, but Kim raised her hand and silenced him.

"I can't believe to you," Kim said as she gave Capo a sad look. She was hurt on the inside and she knew it showed on the outside, but she still had to be strong and remain seated so she wouldn't rip Capo's head off. "I know we may not have the best relationship or I may not be the best woman in the world, but regardless to all that I've always been real with you and straight up," she said as a tear escaped her eye. "You got me feeling so stupid right now. Everybody always tells me to stop dealing with you cause you ain't no good, but stupid Kim. I just stick around and hold you down in any and every situation."

"Fuck what everybody else thinks. All that matters is what you think," Capo countered.

"I don't care about what everybody else thinks. I know that you are no good. You've been no good since I met you," Kim said in a serious tone. "You may be no good, but you're good for me so I could care less what anybody has to say about who I choose to be with, but you could at least put some shade on your shit."

"I'm sorry baby. I wasn't thinking," Capo said. For the first time in his life he felt bad for hurting someone.

"Now every time I come up here these stupid ass officers going to be laughing at me behind my back," Kim said shaking her head with a disgusted look on her face. "I'm out here riding for you, but I need to know that you riding for me."

Capo sat there for a second and let her words sink in. Everything she said made perfectly good sense, but Capo wasn't sure if he was ready to settle down at the moment, but he did know that whenever he did decide to settle down it would definitely be with Kim. "I'm sorry baby," he said as he slid Kim's hands into his and kissed the tips of her fingers gingerly. "Do you forgive me baby?" Capo said giving Kim the sad puppy dog eyes.

Kim sat there for a second and then she finally cracked a smile. "Nigga get over here and play with this pussy; getting me all worked up ready to kill a bitch," she laughed. Truth be told, Kim knew she would never leave Capo. Her love and loyalty ran too deep to ever leave him for dead in somebodies jail.

"I love you," Capo whispered as his hand slipped underneath the table.

"I..I..I love you too," Kim moaned.

22

WHERE AM I

Ashley woke up in a nice sized room and a nice sized bed. She looked around and saw that the room was empty except for the bed that she laid on. She quickly hopped up off the bed and ran to the window and tried to open it, but it was no use. Someone had nailed the windows shut. Next she ran to the door and turned the knob hoping that it would be open, but she had no such luck. Ashley had no idea where she was or if she was going to make it out of this situation alive. On the other side of the door she could hear several different voices having a conversation. She sat back down on the bed and wondered just how long she had left to live before the men on the other side of the door murdered her the same way they had did her mother and father. Ashley stood up and walked back over to the window. She looked out and wondered if Angela would come for her. *"Where are you Angela?"* she said to herself.

The sound of someone entering the room snapped Ashley back into reality. In walked a man dressed in an expensive looking suit. "Sit down!" the man barked. Ashley did as she was told in fear that if she didn't, the man would kill her.

"I'm going to get straight to the point. My name is Frank," he began. "And if you don't tell me where that disk or flash drive is, I'm going to make sure you have a very painful death," he said with a straight face. "Now where's that disk?"

"Angela has it," Ashley told him. "I gave it to her and told her to make copies of whatever was on it so whatever ya'll were trying to hide, the whole world knows about it now," she bluffed. It was a brave move, but also a stupid one.

Frank turned and back slapped Ashley. The slap was so hard that the impact forced her to flip off of the bed. "Let's try this again! Where's that disk?"

Ashley looked at him and said nothing.

Frank sighed loudly as he walked over and kicked Ashley in her face. "If you think I won't kill a kid, you are sadly mistaking," he said shaking his head as he slowly walked towards her again. "I lost my whole world a few weeks ago, so none of this don't mean shit to me!" He stood over her. "Last time I'm going to ask you. Where's that disk?"

Ashley said nothing.

Frank raised his hand to strike Ashley again, but Mr. Clarke's voice stopped him.

"That's enough!" Mr. Clarke said as he entered the room. "Stand down and let me have a word with her alone" he ordered. Frank made sure he bumped shoulders with Mr. Clarke on his way out. Patience wasn't one of his stronger qualities. Frank was into making things happen and not sitting around waiting for things to happen. He felt as if Mr. Clarke was being way too nice to the little girl. If he were in charge, he would of tortured the little girl all night. Frank figured it wouldn't take long to get a child to crack, but Mr. Clarke had shut down his suggestion.

"Listen Ashley, I know you're scared," Mr. Clarke began. "But you have to help me if you want me to help you. I really need to know where that thumb drive is. Can you help me?"

"Angela has it," Ashley said. Thoughts of spitting in Mr. Clarke's face like they did in the movies crossed her mind, but she quickly realized that, that would be a terrible idea.

"Okay do you know where I can find Angela right now?" he asked in a calm tone. Ashley shook her head no.

Mr. Clarke smiled then left the room and locked the door behind him. Out in another room Frank sat in a dark room sipping on Vodka straight out the bottle. Ever since his wife had been killed, he felt like he was literally losing his mind. All day long all he thought about was if he could go back to that day in the supermarket and change how things played out. In Frank's mind it was his fault why his wife was dead. If he would have been protecting her like a husband was supposed to, then his wife would still be here right now, but she wasn't which meant that he had failed. His pain quickly turned into hurt, and then into anger when he began to think about Angela. He may not of had saved his wife, but it was Angela's bullet that had killed her and for that she would have to pay dearly.

"Fuck this!" Frank shot to his feet and headed back to Ashley's room. He was sick and tired of playing games. If Frank wanted a showdown with The Teflon Queen he would have to do something drastic to lure her to him. Before Frank could reach Ashley's room, Mr. Clarke stopped him. "Don't you even think about it," he warned. "Don't worry. Angela will come looking for the girl."

"And how are you so sure about that?" Frank asked. He wasn't with sitting around and waiting for something to happen. He was from the old school where when you didn't have a way, you made a way.

"Because Angela is the best," Mr. Clarke said with a serious look on his face. "But I promise you, we'll be ready for that bitch as soon as she shows up. You want her right?"

"You damn right!" Frank answered.

"Well you better be ready for her because she's definitely coming," Mr. Clarke said and left Frank standing there with something to think about.

***

For the next two days Frank trained and put his body through the ultimate test so he could be ready for Angela when she showed up. Sweat dripped from his shirtless chiseled body as he did push-ups. Not only did he need his mind to be sharp, but he also needed his body to be ready for whatever was to come. In all of Frank's years, he'd never had to take out or go head up with a fellow assassin, but after seeing his wife get murdered, Frank was ready to go all out. Angela would have to pay for what she did. Frank wiped his face with a towel and got his weapons ready. He knew that Mr. Clarke's men would be no match for Angela so he would have to pick up most of the slack. Frank was one of the best hit men out there, but his skills would surely get put to the test and Frank was more than ready to let his skills do the talking for him. When Angela showed up he planned on being well prepared for whatever she had planned.

***

After taking a long shower Frank poured himself a glass of Vodka and began to get dressed. He took another sip from his drink when he heard his cell phone buzz. He quickly picked it up and saw that he had a text message. He looked at the text message that read. *"I'm here."*

Frank walked through the mansion until he reached the front door. He opened the door and saw Spice the Brazilian prostitute standing on the other side of the door wearing nothing but some heels and a trench coat.

"I knew you'd be calling again," Spice smiled. Her lips were painted bright red and so were her finger nails. Frank quickly took Spice up to the room he was staying in. He knew he needed to be on point at all times, but right now he needed to relieve some stress. Frank sat down on the edge of the bed and sipped on his drink. "So," he began. "How have you been?"

"This is how I've been," Spice said removing the trench coat and tossing it down to the floor. The only thing she had on underneath were a pair of black fish net stockings and nothing else. "Is it hot in here or is it just me?"

"It's definitely hot in here," Frank said as he removed his dress shirt while Spice did a seductive dance for him. She stood directly in front of Frank and bent over at the waist and began shaking her ass right in his face. Frank quickly slid down to floor on his knees and gave Spice's pussy a nice long lick.

"You've been waiting to taste this pussy haven't you? Ahhhh, haven't you oooww," Spice purred as she backed her ass up even further into Frank's face. He licked her like she was melting ice cream, licked her like he needed to taste her juices in order to live, licked her like her orgasm was the antidote to his broken heart.

Frank let out a beast like growl as he spun Spice around, lifted her up, and positioned her upside down holding her tightly around the waist.

"Oh my God! Please don't drop me Daddy," Spice said in a husky porn star type of voice as she grabbed a hold of Frank's dick and put it in her mouth and began to slurp on it nice and slow and loud. Spice was upside down in Frank's arms. Her dark hair was hanging to his feet while her thighs locked around both sides of his neck squeezing his neck as his hands held and squeezed her soft ass. Frank savored Spice while she took him in her mouth sucking the shit out of his dick making it a vertical and simultaneous exchange of pleasure. Frank licked and slurped and let his tongue massage Spice's wet peach until he felt her legs tighten around his head and her body shook uncontrollably. Spice fired off several curse words as Frank slurped her pussy clean.

Frank roughly tossed Spice down on to the bed, her body bouncing up and down. Frank positioned her flat on her stomach and quickly crawled over top of her and enter her from behind.

"Ahhh yes fuck this pussy! Ahh fuck this pussy and make me cum all over that dick!" Spice growled. She frowned back at what was going in and out of her. She stared at it with moans and detachment. Frank fucked Spice hard and rough, fucked her like he was fucking his wife, fucked her like that was his pussy, fucked her like he was trying to ruin her insides. Spice then aggressively flipped Frank over and got on top. She squatted over him and used the head board for support. She violently bounced up and down on Frank's dick as she screamed loudly. Spice made sounds like she was dying a painful death. Her skin slapping against his sounded like the ultimate battle. "Oh My Fucking God!!" Spice screamed at the top of her lungs as she arched her back and came a long drawn out orgasm, her moans never ending.

Frank tossed Spice off of him, stood straight up on the bed, and shoved his dick in Spice's mouth trying to hit the back of her throat. "Drain this dick right now!" he demanded. Spice grabbed Frank's dick with two hands and began twisting both her hands at a steady rhythm as she sloppily slurped all over Frank's dick. Spice jerked Frank's dick back and forth and spit on it then quickly sucked it off. Spice sloppily spit on Frank's dick again. She took him in her mouth. Felt his hands in her hair and his penis at the back of her throat.

"Oooooooh shit!!!" Frank grunted as he pushed deeper and came. He watched as Spice sloppily and noisily slurped every last drop out the tip of his dick.

Once Frank's duty was done he handed Spice double what she charged.

"Thanks baby," Spice said licking her lips in a slutty manner. It was a filthy gesture but for some strange reason, it seemed to turn Frank on. "Will I be seeing you again?" Spice asked.

"God willing," Frank said and sent Spice on her way. Now that, that was over he had to focus and figure out the best way to take Angela out without getting himself killed in the process. He knew going head up with Angela would be like a high speed chess match, but in this game he was the king.

23

I'M GOING IN

Detective Washington pulled onto a dark street and hit the lights. For the past week he had been doing a lot of research on this Mr. Clarke person and he came to find out that the man had his hands in a little bit of everything, and he was definitely considered a player. A lot of thoughts had been running through Detective Washington's mind as he tried to figure out what was what and who was who. Never in a million years would he have ever thought that he would be working with a wanted assassin, but now here he was working hand and hand with a well-known cop killer. Detective Washington knew Angela was supposed to be one of the bad guys, but when in her presence she genuinely felt like one of the good guys. She didn't seem like the ruthless killer that he had read about, but instead she carried herself as a person who did what they had to do. Detective Washington's train of thought was snapped out of when he spotted a figure dressed in all black with a black hood covering their head walking at a quick pace towards his car. The passenger door opened and the figure in all black sat down in the passenger seat and slammed the door shut.

"Did you find anything out about Mr. Clarke?" Angela asked with the strings on her hood drawn tight. Detective Washington handed Angela a folder.

"Yeah he definitely seems like a player," he told her. "He seems to have his hands in a little bit of everything, extortion, politics, stocks, and even a bit of prostitution."

Angela didn't respond. Instead she just looked over the paperwork that sat inside the folder. Inside the paperwork she saw that Mr. Clarke owned a mansion out in Denver Colorado. "Here's where they're keeping Ashley," she pointed to the picture of the mansion.

"How do you know?"

"I just know." Angela snapped. "I'm going after her."

"We can't just go to his mansion and look around. We'll need a warrant for that," Detective Washington said.

"No you'll need a warrant. I'm not a cop," Angela reminded him.

"But I want you to have some back up if you go out there," Detective Washington said. "You know that mansion will be crawling with armed security out the ass."

"I'm going after Ashley," Angela said ignoring everything Detective Washington just said. "Listen once I get there, gunfire is sure to follow. Once the war pops off you and your team of cops can come and help me and I'll just make sure I vanish before you cops can arrest me," she said with a smirk.

"Too dangerous," Detective Washington said shaking his head. "My men will shoot on sight when they see you."

"So will I," she countered. Angela knew the mission that lied ahead wouldn't be an easy one. She knew there was a chance that she could be killed and she also knew that there was a chance that Ashley was already dead.

"I'll back you up however I can," Detective Washington said. He knew Angela was about to go on a suicide mission and he wished it was something he could do that would help. "I just wish me and my men had a reason to run up in that mansion."

"Here's your reason right here," Angela handed Detective Washington the thumb drive. "Whatever is on this thumb drive must be very important if so many people had to lose their lives over it"

Detective Washington studied the thumb drive closely. "Why did you give this to me?"

"You helped me by not locking me up so now I'm just returning the favor," Angela smiled. "Whatever is on the thumb drive is sure to put someone in jail for a very long time."

Detective Washington stuck the thumb drive down in his pocket and then turned and faced Angela. "Thank you," he said.

Angela smiled. "Don't mention it."

"You be careful and good luck," Detective Washington smiling.

"I don't need luck."

"Go save that little girl," Detective Washington told her.

"I will," Angela said and then exited the car and disappeared in the shadows of the darkness. She had a lot of work to do and she couldn't wait to get started.

*****

Detective Washington sat behind his desk with his eyes locked on his computer screen. He had been trying to gain access to the thumb drive for hours. At first he was having a hard time but after a few hours he finally figured it out. "Bingo!" Detective Washington said in a happy tone. His eyes were burning and he badly wanted to go home. Once Detective Washington gained access, he was surprised to see a video on his computer screen. Without hesitation he pressed play. What played out on the screen were two people tied and bounded to two different chairs; a male and a female. On the video Detective Washington could clearly hear the woman begging and pleading. "Baby please don't do this." Then suddenly another man walked into the screen shot. It was Mr. Clarke and in his hand he was holding something. He smoothly walked up to the man and woman and began to pour what looked like gasoline on both of their heads. The man and woman both shook their heads frantically. Mr. Clarke then turned and faced the camera and shouted, "Hey Randy give me a light and make sure you get all this on tape so I can watch this bitch die over and over!" Whoever was holding the camera stretched their arm out and handed Mr. Clarke a book of matches.

"Baby I'm sorry it was a mistake!" the woman yelled out just as Mr. Clarke strikes a match and tossed it on top of the woman's head. The flames quickly engulfed as the woman screamed to the top of her lungs. Mr. Clarke then walked over towards the man, struck a match, and watched as his body too engulfed into flames. Both the man and woman screamed for a few more seconds as their skin melted right off of their bodies. Then suddenly the recording stoped.

"Holy Shit!!!" Detective Washington said to no one in particular. What he had was way more than enough the get a warrant to go search Mr. Clarke's home and detain him. He quickly opened up his files and scanned through them. In a file it stated that Mr. Clarke's wife had been killed in a bad car crash along with a male friend of hers. Detective Washington swiftly hopped up from his seat and headed to his boss's house. If everything worked out the way he planned, he'd be able to get a warrant and have his men in Denver in time to help Angela and maybe even save little Ashley.

"So Randy must of knew Mr. Clarke was going to kill him so he made a copy of the murder tape as insurance to stay alive," Detective Washington said to himself as he flew down the highway doing 90 miles per hour.

24

I'M TIRED OF YOU

Capo breathed heavily as he dropped down from the pull up bar. Ever since he had gotten locked up, Capo had been working hard on building his body up. He had been doing that because he didn't have much else to do. On the inside Capo still felt bad about what he had done to Kim. She was good girl. The problem was he didn't know how to be a good man or how to treat a woman for that matter. The good thing about the whole situation was he had a lot of time to improve in all the areas he was lacking. Capo went down and did some pushups and when he came up he saw Wayne standing in front of him. Capo's first thought was that Wayne must have wanted trouble, so he got in a good position where he could steal on him and knock him out.

"I didn't come here for all that," Wayne said quickly taking a step back. "I just came to talk."

"Step the fuck off!" Capo said dismissing him. "Me and you ain't got shit to talk about."

"I just wanted to come over here and tell you that I love you like a son. I always have and always will" Wayne told him. "I came over to see if we could maybe renew our friendship. I miss how we used to be."

Capo hopped back up on the bar and continued on with his work out as if Wayne wasn't even there.

"Listen Capo I have a business proposition for you," Wayne said leaning in and whisperig. "I need your help and we can both get paid."

"Fuck outta here," Capo said waving him off. "Why don't you go get one of your Muslim brothers to help you out," he said with a smirk as he dropped down and began his push-ups.

"I hired the Muslims for protection, but this is business and besides you know those Muslims be trying to act like they're so righteous. I need someone that I know I can trust," Wayne said. "Somebody that knows how to get money, somebody that ain't afraid to go out and get it."

"Stop beating around the bush" Capo huffed. "How much is the job paying and what do you need me to do?"

"Listen," Wayne said looking over both shoulders before he spoke any further. "All I need you to do is have someone drop something off with one of my people's once a month."

"How does this work?" Capo asked. He wasn't the type to turn down free money.

"I'll have someone drop a package off to your peoples and all they have to do is drop it off to someone else," Wayne said making it sound so simple. "Each drop off is paying ten thousand."

"What's the catch?" Capo asked. He knew this deal sounded a little too good to be true, not to mention his trust level for Wayne wasn't as high as it used to be. He wanted to be sure that Wayne wasn't trying to jam him up.

"No catch," Wayne smiled. "Listen Capo I don't want no drama with you. I got nothing but love for you and I just want us back on the same team."

"A'ight give me a few days and I'll think about it," Capo said then spun off leaving Wayne standing there alone.

Capo wasn't sure of what to make of the proposition that Wayne made to him. One part of him felt as if he shouldn't trust Wayne, while another part of him felt as if he could use the money and he knew that Kim could definitely use the money. Capo's plan was to go to his cell and think about it for the next two days and then give Wayne an answer. As Capo headed back to his cell he thought about all the good times that him and Wayne had and all the fun times the two shared together. Out of all the years of doing business with Wayne, Capo couldn't think of one time that the man ever did any funny business.

Capo's thoughts were rudely interrupted when he stepped foot in his cell. In his cell his cellmate sat on the toilet taking a shit. Capo's face immediately crumbled up when the foul odor assaulted his nostrils. "Damn nigga flush that shit!" he barked.

"I ain't finished yet," his cellmate countered matching Capo's tone. He was sick and tired of Capo talking to him like a child. He had a shank hidden under his pillow and he planned on using it on Capo as soon as he got done handling his business on the toilet.

"Nigga why is you sitting on top of shit? Flush that shit! You got the whole cell smelling crazy!" Capo fumed.

"Nigga I'll flush it when I get done!" his cellmate capped back.

"So you ain't gon flush that shit?" Capo asked. Before his cell mate even got a chance to reply, Capo had already stole on him. He wasn't the type to go back and forth with a clown over some dumb shit. The punch stunned his cell mate, knocking him clean off the toilet bowl.

"Nigga! Don't you ever talk...like you built like that! Faggot!" Capo barked and each time he stomped his cell mate's face even further into the floor.

"Clown!" Capo shouted and gave the man one last stomp. He stood back and looked at his cellmate laying on the floor unconscious with his ass hanging out. He walked over to the toilet and flushed it. Capo then grabbed his cellmate by the ankles and dragged him out of the cell, leaving him lying unconscious on the tier. Once the rest of the inmates saw the unconscious man sprawled across the tier with his ass hanging out they immediately began going crazy, yelling, and screaming with excitement.

Two minutes later four officers came and surrounded Capo's cell. Already knowing the procedure, Capo turned around, placed his hands behind his back, and stuck them through the small slot so the officers could place the cuffs on his wrist. From there the officers escorted Capo straight to the box where he would be staying for the next few months.

25

IT'S NOT A GAME

"That motherfucker tried to blow my head off!" Bone huffed as he poured himself a shot of Patron. "It was a whole army of them."

"I told you his crew was deep out here," Mya said downing the liquid fire that sat in her cup in one gulp. "We have to figure out a way to take Scarface out once and for all."

"Yeah I know," Bone said downing another shot. He knew Scarface had the upper hand because he was in his city right now. "We need to figure out a way to catch this fucker off guard." The more Bone thought about the situation, the more it pissed him off. This whole beef started over Shekia. Bone put Shekia to sleep and Scarface called himself coming to her rescue and now here they were.

"The way to get at Scarface is to go through his girl Shekia," Mya told him. Deep down inside she was still mad that Scarface had refused to get rid of Shekia for her. Shekia had thrown a monkey wrench in her game plan. Mya had planned on using Scarface and in the end taking everything he had. Now Mya just wanted Scarface dead. She was afraid that when he finally ran into her that he would definitely kill her.

"He still with that raggedy bitch Shekia?" Bone asked remembering how he had violated her.

"Yup," Mya said with a hint of jealousy in her voice. After she was rescued from the back of Scarface's truck, she planned on going to Scarface's house and violating Shekia, but after staking out at her house for a few days, she realized that no one was at the house. "I can't stand that bitch!" she spat.

"How do we find her?" Bone asked. He was sick and tired of playing games with Mya. All he wanted to do was find out where Scarface or Shekia was and handle his business. Bone was tired of fucking and doing sexual favors for the little bit of information that Mya was providing.

"What's in it for me?" Mya asked in a slutty tone.

"What you want?" Bone asked with a phony smile on his face. Mya removed her boy shorts and spread her legs open wide. "Oh you know what I want."

Bone snatched Mya from off the couch and lifted her up like she had the weight of a baby. He lifted her high with her legs opening, resting on both sides of his neck and the heat of her vagina in his face. Bone expertly licked and sucked on Mya's clit. They stumbled toward the wall. The wall was stopping Mya from falling to the floor. Bone held her up, felt one of her hands on his head, heard the other grabbing at the white wall, slapping the wall until she found her balance. Her hands were sliding and knocking glass-framed pictures off the wall. Photos were crashind down to the floor and glass was breaking. Bone's lips and tongue were pressed against her pussy. Mya's weight pressed down on his mouth. She moved on the hardness of his chin, moved on his chin as she held him tightly and moaned. She gyrated and grind on his face. "Ooooooh My God!!!" Mya yelled as she wrapped her legs around the back of Bone's neck and announced her orgasm. After her eruption Mya went limp in Bone's arms. She arched her back and threw her head back with her head hanging down lifeless.

Bone quickly put Mya down and roughly and forcefully entered her from behind. She held her breath for a moment. Her nostrils flared, her back arched, and her legs tightened. She let out a slow, pain-filled sigh. Bone plunged in and out of Mya at a fast pace. His moan was abrupt and guttural. Bone sank deep, came out and sank deep again. Each pump was more intense than the last. Each moan was louder and each stroke devastating.

Bone moved deeper inside Mya. He held her waist, made her sit, tried to fill her up, and make her feel every inch of his hardness. He wanted to fuck the life out of her, wanted to fuck her brains out, wanted to fuck her into a coma. Bone roughly snatched Mya up to her feet and tossed her against the wall. He stayed behind her and dipped to get a good angel. He pressed her breast flat against the wall thrusting in and out of her deep and steady. Mya took her right foot and wrapped it around Bone from behind and then did the same with her left foot. He held her up as she craned her neck, reached for his face, and kissed it. Bone fucked Mya like he hated her, like he wanted to hurt her, until he finally exploded inside of Mya.

"Argh!" Bone groaned as he emptied himself inside of her box.

"I know you didn't just cum inside me!" Mya said with an attitude. "You know you didn't have a condom on!"

Bone sighed as he grabbed the bottle Ciroc from off the coffee table by the neck. "My bad," he said easing from behind Mya.

"I swear to God, I better not get pregnant!" Mya continued her rant. When she turned around, Bone busted the bottle over her head sending a spray of broken glass all over the place.

"Shut the fuck up bitch!" Bone said as he broke out in a drunken laugh. He was tired of playing games with Mya. She was playing with the wrong one.

"Why are you doing this?" Mya asked as blood leaked from a gash in her head. Bone cocked his leg back and kicked Mya in the face causing her head to jerk back violently.

"Asking me why this and why that," Bone spoke out loud to no one in particular. He kneeled down and placed the sharp, rugged end of the bottle up to Mya's neck. "Bitch you got five seconds to tell me everything you know about Scarface and Shekia!" Bone growled. For the next ten minutes he listened to Mya spill her guts telling him everything he needed and wanted to know about Scarface and Shekia. Once Mya was done spilling her guts, Bone jabbed the broken bottle in her neck and watched her bleed out. Before Bone left he made sure he cleaned out Mya's pocketbook just for the hell of it.

When Bone stepped outside Mya's crib, he slid right into the Benz that awaited him curbside.

"How'd it go?" Mike Murder asked with a smirk.

"Like taking candy from a baby," Bone replied with a smile.

"I was sick and tired of that bitch playing games," Mike Murder said shaking his head. He wasn't the one for all of the games. If he was Bone, Mya would have been dead a long time ago. "What's the next move?"

"We kill Scarface and that bitch Shekia," Bone said as the two men busted out laughing.

26

I LOVE YOU.

Shekia sat on the couch at her best friend Sandy's house crying her eyes out. She loved Scarface to death, but being with him was beginning to be too dangerous. One day everything was cool and the next day someone was shooting up her house. When Scarface got out of jail he promised Shekia that he would no longer be participating in any type of street activity and three days later their house was being shot up. Shekia was afraid that the next time she wouldn't be so lucky. She was afraid that the next time a shootout took place that her and the baby that she was carrying in her stomach would end up on the receiving end of a stray bullet and that was a risk that she wasn't willing to take. There wasn't a love in this world that was worth dying for or losing her child for that matter. The more Shekia thought about the situation, the more she cried, and the more she was finally starting to realize that Scarface was never going to change. He would never be the type of man that she wanted and needed. The streets had a strong hold on him. The hold was so strong that not only was it bringing him down, but Shekia was afraid that it might pull her down as well.

"Girl I don't even know why you crying over that sorry, no good ass nigga," Sandy said in a salty tone. She was the queen of the man bashers. When any one of her friends were having man problems, her first suggestion was to leave the man alone because all men were no good in her eyes. "All he gon do is call back talking all that bullshit about how he gon change and how he'll never hurt you again," Sandy said shaking her head. "That's what's wrong with women today. They all think that they *"need"* a man so they put up with all their bullshit hoping and praying that one day their man will figure it out and get it right."

"But Scarface is different," Shekia said, but Sandy quickly cut her off.

"You see that's your problem right there." Sandy gave Shekia a sad look. "Every woman seems to think that they man is different. Shiiiiddd," she said drawing out the word. "The only thing different are they're names and sometimes those aren't even different," she huffed.

"Well I don't know what type of men you used to dealing with, but Scarface ain't like that," Shekia said in a matter of fact tone.

"Child please," Sandy said waving Shekia off. "His name is Scarface. That's enough said," Sandy said and began dying laughing at her own joke. All Shekia could do was shake her head. This was just the reason why she hated telling Sandy when something was going wrong in her and Scarface's relationship. Sandy had been cheated on and dogged out so many times that in her mind all men were dogs, but the truth of the matter was all her life Sandy kept on dealing with the same type of man over and over expecting different types of results.

"Well all men aren't the same," Shekia said and left it at that. Sometimes she just needed someone to listen and not give an opinion all the time.

"I'm sorry girl," Sandy said catching on to Shekia's attitude. "You know I got nothing but love for you. I just hate to see you go through shit like this because I know you're a good woman."

"I understand," Shekia said as the tears began to flow again. Sandy embraced her, giving her a tight hug. She hated to have to see her best friend go through all this, but at the moment all she could do was be there for her girl.

"Don't worry, things are going to get greater, later," she told Shekia. Sandy had to calm down, because she was beginning to get pissed off as if she was the one in the relationship taking the abuse. "How about we go out and get a drink?"

"No can do!"

Sandy laughed. "What you pregnant or something?" When Shekia didn't answer she knew that things had quickly gone from bad to worse. "Noooo Shekia, please tell me that you're not pregnant?" she asked with a suspicious raised brow.

Shekia's tears only confirmed what Sandy had already assumed. "I need a drink!" Sandy stormed over to the kitchen and a minute later returned with a glass of wine in her hand. "Girl what have you been over there doing with yourself?"

"I had just found out that I was pregnant right before my car accident," Shekia told her. "At first I was happy about it, but then Scarface came home and told me that he'd been hanging around his ex...."

"Niggaz keep a side bitch sniffing around," Sandy said cutting in and rolling her eyes.

"But now I don't know what to do," Shekia said. "I love Scarface to death. He's a good man, but I'm just afraid that he may be here today and gone tomorrow."

"What you need to do is get you a *"real"* man and stop fucking with them stupid ass street niggaz," Sandy spat. The more Shekia told her, the more upset Sandy was becoming.

A loud knock at the door startled the two women. Sandy walked to the door and snatched it open with an attitude. Seeing Scarface standing on the other side of the door only pissed Sandy off even further. "What are you doing here and what do you want?" she asked sucking her teeth.

"I need to talk to Shekia. I know she's here," Scarface huffed. He hated the fact that he even had to have a conversation with the man hating chick, but at the moment he didn't have a choice.

"She doesn't want to talk to you right now so why don't you just step the fuck off!" Sandy went to shut the door in his face, but Scarface quickly jammed his boot in the door before it could close.

"Look bitch, stop playing! I need to speak to Shekia!" Scarface said forcing his way inside the apartment. "Shekia where you at!?" he yelled throughout the house.

"Get out of my house right now before I call the police," Sandy threatened as she pulled out her cell phone.

Scarface was about to go off on Sandy, until Shekia showed up. "Put that phone down," Shekia told Sandy and then turned and faced Scarface. "What are you doing here and what do you want?" she said rolling her eyes at Scarface.

"We need to talk," Scarface barked as he grabbed Shekia's hand and led her outside. He was sick and tired of playing games with her. He needed to know what was what.

"What?" Shekia said with her arms folded across her chest as she purposely avoided eye contact with Scarface.

"So this what we doing; the back and forth thing?"

"I'm not doing anything," Shekia countered.

"So that's it? We over just like that?"

"Scarface we've had this discussion over and over again and honestly I'm sick and tired of fighting and going back and forth with you about the same thing," Shekia told him. "And honestly if I don't leave, things are never going to change."

"Never going to change?" Scarface repeated. "I've changed everything for you! I told you that I was done with all that street shit!"

"Yeah that's what you told me, but what you showing me is two different things," Shekia spat.

"You ain't give me a chance to show you anything," Scarface countered. He knew that if he wanted to get Shekia back, he would definitely have his work cut out for him especially since she had been talking to Sandy for hours. "Why don't you come back home so we can talk?"

"Come back home so we can talk or come back home so I can get shot?" she said sarcastically. "I don't even feel safe around you. A man is supposed to make a woman feel safe and protected and I don't feel that with you."

"I would never let anything happen to you and you know it," Scarface said defensively. He may have not been the best man in the world, but one thing he took pride in was taking care of and protecting Shekia. "Baby come home please..."

"I can't," Shekia said looking down at the ground. "I can't live like this no more."

"It's because I might be going back to jail isn't it?" Scarface asked. "Be honest."

Shekia looked at him like he was insane. "I don't believe you just said that."

"Well that's how it feels."

"Well it's good to know how you really feel about me," Shekia said shaking her head. The fact that Scarface could possibly be facing some time had nothing to do with why she no longer wanted to be in a relationship with him. The truth was this wasn't the type of life that she wanted to bring a child into.

"I'm just saying everything was fine until I got locked up and then all of a sudden you started to change," Scarface said. "What's up with that?"

"I'm pregnant!"

Scarface stood for a second to let what Shekia had just told him register. Out of all the things that he had going on in his life, this was the best news he'd received in a long time. A part of Scarface was happy and another part of him was sad. He was happy that Shekia was pregnant and carrying his baby, but he was sad that she was carrying his baby, but no longer wanted to be with him. "So you gon 'up and leave me while you're carrying my baby?"

"It's not like that."

"Then what's it like?"

"I don't want to live like this no more!" Shekia yelled as tears streamed down her face. "You almost got me and your child killed the other day! I'm scared! I'm scared that one night you won't make it home! I'm scared that one day I'll have to explain to our child why his father is gone and he's never coming back!"

"Listen," Scarface said. "Me being a father is one thing you never have to worry about and what you need to realize is that I'm trying to turn my life around and that takes time."

"Well I don't have no more time," Shekia capped back.

"That's your word?" Scarface asked. "So that's it. You just gon give up on me when I'm trying?"

"I don't want to do this no more," Shekia cried. Scarface looked at Shekia, turned and left her standing there alone. Her words had just crushed and taken the life right out of him. He couldn't believe what Shekia had just told him and deep down inside he still felt that her sudden change of attitude had to do with the murder charges that he was facing. He slowly walked over to his car, hopped in, and pulled off. That was it. Scarface and Shekia were officially done. From here on out she no longer existed to him. He would now have to cut all ties with Shekia and flush her out of his system once and for all and move on with his life. It would be a hard thing to do, but this was something that had to be done.

***

Shekia stormed back into Sandy's apartment and cried her eyes out. She knew that once Scarface had walked off they were officially done and that there was no coming back. Of course she loved him, but at the end of the day she knew that her being with him wasn't safe. Things were beginning to spiral out of control and she just hoped and prayed that Scarface could get out before it was too late.

Sandy sat hugging Shekia and rubbing her back while she cried on her shoulder. If she could she would have kicked Scarface's ass for hurting her friend the way he did. As the two woman sat hugging, a loud knock at the door caught them off guard.

"Tell Scarface that I don't want to talk to or see him right now," Shekia sobbed.

"I got you girl," Sandy said hopping to her feet and rushing towards the door. She couldn't wait to curse Scarface the fuck out for upsetting her friend like this. Sandy snatched the door open ready to act a fool when instead of Scarface standing on the other side of the door she saw two men dressed in all black. "Ummm, can I help y'all?"

Mike Murder roughly pushed his way through the door sending Sandy stumbling back inside the apartment. Before Sandy had a chance to protest Bone had back slapped Sandy down to the floor with the butt of his gun knocking her out cold. Bone stood over Sandy, raised his leg, and stomped down on her head. Her unconscious body jerked from the impact.

Mike Murder entered the living room and spotted Shekia sitting on the couch with a shocked and scared look on her face. "Is this the bitch right here?" he yelled over his shoulder. When

Shekia saw Bone step into the living room she almost shitted on herself.

"You don't look happy to see me," Bone smiled. Shekia looked a little different from the last time he'd seen her. She had gained a little weight and she wore her hair in a different style.

"Bone I don't know what you're thinking but I don't have nothing to do with what you and Scarface got going on," she said with her hands up in surrender.

"You have everything to do with this," Bone replied. His plan was to hit Scarface where it hurt and that was in his heart.

"Bone listen you don't have to do this," Shekia said as tears ran down her face. "You never used to be like this. When me, you, Capo, and Kim were working together we were like a family."

"Bitch fuck you, Kim, and Capo! Ain't none of y'all no family of mines," Bone spat. "Where's Scarface?"

"Bone I'm pregnant," Shekia pleaded. "Please don't hurt me or my baby... Please..."

Bone looked Shekia in the eyes. "Not my problem," he said as he fired a bullet into her chest. Him and Mike Murder watched as she wheezed and tried to breath. Shekia sat wide eyed as her entire shirt turned dark red. She couldn't believe what was happening. She couldn't believe that she had just been shot, couldn't believe that her life was draining from her body. Where was Scarface when she needed him? Why was this happening to her?

Bone stood over Shekia, shook his head and put a bullet in her head splattering blood all over the wall. "Fuck that bitch," he said as him and Mike Murder made their exit leaving Shekia lying dead on the couch.

***

Scarface sat at the red light cursing Shekia out in his mind. He couldn't believe how she could say the things that she had said to him. It was as if all the improvement that he was making was going unnoticed by her and she was the only reason that he was trying to change. Scarface also knew that Shekia's man bashing friend Sandy had put a lot of bullshit in her head, because that's what she did best. It was always the ones who didn't have a man that always tried to tell you how to have a successful relationship or someone who didn't have a dollar in their pocket trying to give you financial advice. The more Scarface thought about the situation, the more furious he was becoming. "Fuck!" he cursed as he hit a U-turn and headed back towards Sandy's apartment. A part of him wanted nothing to do with Shekia and another part of him wouldn't allow himself to go out like that especially while she was carrying his baby in her stomach. Scarface decided to put his pride to the side and man up for his child. The last thing he wanted to do was look like he was bowing down to Shekia's demands, but at the moment this whole situation was bigger than Scarface and Shekia. It was about the unborn child that floated around in her stomach. When Scarface pulled up and saw the apartment door left wide open he immediately knew that something was wrong. He snatched his 9mm from off the front seat and ran inside the apartment. The first thing he saw when he stepped inside the apartment was Sandy sprawled out in the middle of the floor with a bullet hole in her throat. Her eyes were staring up at the ceiling. "Oh my God! Nooo!" Scarface said as he moved on throughout the apartment and found Shekia lying dead on the couch with her brains blow all over the wall. Scarface walked over and rubbed Shekia's stomach as he just stood there and cried. It was as if his entire world had come crashing down in a matter of seconds. "I love you," he whispered looking down at Shekia's lifeless body. Scarface knew that this was all his fault. If he would have just listened to Shekia from the beginning and dealt with the whole Bone situation alone from the beginning none of this would even be going on right now. "I'm sorry," he whispered as he cried like a baby. It was as if his feet were stuck in place and he couldn't move. Scarface dropped down to his knees and hugged Shekia's lifeless body. This was the last time that he'd ever be able to hug her again. As Scarface sat hugging Shekia he heard several footsteps entering the apartment. Thinking it was Bone and his goons, he turned and aimed his gun and fired.

Several police officers stormed in the living room. "Drop the weapon! Sir, drop the weapon!" they yelled before opening fire on Scarface, filling his body with bullets. Scarface's body rocked and moved from side to side until the police were sure that he was dead. Scarface lay dead with his head on Shekia's lap.

27

NO TURNING BACK

Mr. Clarke paced back and forth chain smoking cigarette after cigarette while Ashley sat at the dining room table eating dinner. Several armed guards stood close by just in case little Ashley began to feel a little froggy. The more time that passed, the more Mr. Clarke worried about not having that thumb drive in his possession. He knew what was on the thumb drive could put him away for the rest of his life and that's what worried him the most. The fact that a total stranger held his life in their hands didn't sit well with him.

"Why don't you sit down before you give yourself a heart attack," Frank said entering the dining area.

"Well I'd take a heart attack over spending the rest of my life in jail any day," Mr. Clarke countered.

"Well if Angela ever decides to show up we have men all over the property," Frank told him.

"You think I should leave the country?"

"For what?"

"Just in case that thumb drive falls into the wrong hands, you know?" Mr. Clarke asked in an undecided tone.

"Yeah I think you should leave first thing in the morning just to be on the safe side and let me kill the little girl," Frank suggested. Really all he wanted to do was kill the little girl because he knew it would hurt Angela and he wanted her to hurt the way she made him hurt when she murdered his wife.

Mr. Clarke thought on it for a second. "Fuck it; if Angela doesn't show up tonight the little girl is all yours." As soon as the words left his mouth, all the lights in the mansion went out. About twenty seconds later the backup generator kicked in and lit the entire mansion back up.

"She's here!" Frank said as he pulled his 9mm from his holster with a snap. "Keep a close eye on the girl!" he ordered as he went to go see what was going on.

***

Two guards patrolled the front area of the mansion. They weren't the best guards money could buy, but they were decent. The problem was they had been guarding the front of the mansion for so many years without an incident that they began slacking on the job.

"Hey Sam I'll be right back. I'm going to take a leak," Ryan said as he headed inside the mansion. Once he was gone Sam heard a light splash in the beautiful lake that rest two hundred yards from the front of the mansion.

"What the fuck was that?" Sam said to himself as he went to go check out the noise. As he reached the lake, something inside of him said that something wasn't right. He leaned over and looked down into the water to see if a fish or something would be swimming around. As he looked closer down into the water his reflection stared back at him. Without warning a figure dressed in all black sprang from the water and jammed a knife deep into the side of Sam's neck and then quickly snatched him back down into the water with them.

Minutes later Ryan returned from the bathroom and stepped foot outside and was shocked to see that Sam was nowhere to be found. "Sam!" he called out. "Quit fucking around! Where are you!?"

A masked head broke the lake's surface, peering around to ensure that nobody was watching. Confident that the struggle hadn't been noticed, the black-clad assassin quickly pulled itself from the water, holding an M-4 rifle in their hands. Angela looked through the scope and waited until Ryan was in between the cross hairs before pulling the trigger. The bullet made Ryan's head explode like a melon. His body collapsed seconds later.

Dressed in an all black ninja suit Angela tossed the M-4 over her shoulder and ran full speed towards the mansion. Instead of using the front door, Angela decided to climb up the side of the house and creep through one of the windows. Angela jumped up and began climbing using the same technique she did when rock climbing. Her fingers reached out and found a hole. She pulled herself higher with her other hand while her feet probed for a new cranny. Once Angela reached the window, she quickly pulled herself inside just as another guard patrolled the area where she just was. Inside the room that Angela climbed into, it was dark. Angela took a second to let her eyes adjust to the darkness. Before she took a step through the room, the sound of loud sirens blaring could be heard. Angela quickly rushed over towards the window and peeked out. An entire convoy of police cars and F.B.I trucks came to a screeching halt directly in front of the mansion. Immediately Mr. Clarke's men opened fire on the police setting off a serious gun battle. Once Angela spotted the police, she knew that was Detective Washington giving her back up, which only meant she had a little bit of time to find Ashley and escape the mansion. Angela crept out the room and eased out into the hallway where she spotted three guards standing at the end of the hallway enjoying a good joke. Angela aimed her M-4 in their direction and fired off three shots killing all three of the men instantly with head shots. Angela continued on throughout the mansion. She rounded the corner and ran across three more guards. Again she raised her M-4 at the first gunman's face and pulled the trigger killing the man before he even knew what had hit him. By the time either of the two other guards registered what was happening; Angela had already fired off another shot at the second guard. The guard was clawing at the bullet wound that had just exploded through his sternum like magic. The third man was raising his rifle defensively when a bullet ripped through his left eye. He collapsed without getting a single shot off, having never seen his killer or heard anything besides the briefest of whistling as the bullet sliced through the air on its way to his face. Angela continued to move throughout the mansion making little to no noise what so ever.

Another guard strolled through the halls as the sound of loud gun fire erupted from the ground floor. He quickly ran towards the action and then stopped short when he spotted one of his fellow henchmen lying dead on the floor. As he stood to inspect the man's wounds, a blinding shriek of pain shot through his right lung and he found himself gasping for breath as he fumbled with his rifle. Before his brain could even figure out what was happening, Angela slid behind him and slit his throat.

Angela crept through the mansion, but then stopped short when a room door came flying open. It was a door to a room that she didn't even know existed. An armed guard quickly ran pass her and towards the sound of gunfire, eager to engage in the gun battle. Angela dropped down to one knee and aimed at the moving target. The bullet caught him in mid-stride and he gurgled as he fell, and then moaned before laying still. Angela hoped that nobody had heard him, but then saw the same room door open again and another figure exited holding a rifle. In a fluid motion she pulled a throwing knife from the small of her back and sent it whistling towards his head. The knife caught him in the jaw and stabbed through his mouth, protruding through the back of his head and imbedding itself in the wooden wall behind him. He screamed, a jarring raw sound, prompting Angela to launch another knife at him, this one piercing his heart.

As Angela went to stand up two more gunmen came running up the stairs. Not having too much of a choice, Angela quickly sprinted inside the room that the two men that she'd just killed came out of as bullets tore through the wall right above her head.

The tallest out of the two gunmen entered the room first. Once through the door, there was almost no light, so they waited a few seconds for their eyes to adjust to the darkness. A sound came from further in the depths of the room. The lead man pointed at the light switch. His partner shook his head, no. Light would make them sitting ducks. Right now they had the same darkness to contend with as their adversary. The gunmen knew they weren't dealing with an amateur so they moved with caution. The door opposite them burst wide open as Angela exploded from the storage closet in a blur. The first gunman hardly registered her arrival when he dropped his weapon. Blood leaked down his back from where she had driven the sharp blade into his heart from behind. Angela held the man's body up and grabbed his hand that still held his gun in it. She quickly squeezed the trigger pumping the gunman's partner full of holes. The black ninja suit she wore made it hard for the gunmen to locate her in the dimly lit area. Angela picked up one of the gunmen's assault rifles from off the floor and exited the room. With a big gun fight having broken out, Angela knew that she had to move fast if she wanted to save Ashley. With all the gunfire that was going on, she just hoped and prayed that Ashley was still alive and in one piece.

Angela moved throughout the mansion like a lost puppy. She had no clue where she was heading and with all the rooms in the mansion there was no way she would have time to check all of them. If Angela planned on saving Ashley she would have to come up with a plan. As she crept throughout the mansion, a man twice her size appeared out of nowhere and caught her with a rabbit punch to the back of her head. The punch stunned Angela and caused her to drop her weapon. Before she got a chance to recover, the big man was all over her. He threw a three punch combination and two of the blows landed flush on Angela's chin, but she was able to weave the last one. The big man charged Angela running full speed. He didn't want to allow her a chance to get herself together. The big man hit Angela hard lifting her up off her feet as the two went crashing down the stairs. Angela and the big man tumbled and flipped over and over again until finally reaching the bottom landing. Fortunately for Angela she landed on top of the big man. The big man reached his arms out and went to strangle Angela, but a knife being shoved into his Adam's apple put an end to all of that.

Angela winced in pain as she stood to her feet and pulled a silenced .380 from her holster and continued on throughout the mansion. On Angela's right she spotted a cop spring from behind a wall with a rifle in his hand. Without thinking twice Angela fired once in his direction and put him down with a shot to the throat. She had one mission to accomplish and she wasn't leaving that mansion until she accomplished it.

***

Ashley sat still at the dining room table as a gun fight between Mr. Clarke's men and the police broke out. She didn't know what was going on, but whatever it was it had to be bad by the way Mr. Clarke and his people were panicking. One of the guards roughly grabbed Ashley by the collar of her shirt and yanked her up to her feet. "Move!" he barked, as he rushed Ashley down the hall. Ashley slowed her pace a bit and when the guard went to give her another shove, Ashley surprised him. She swiftly snatched the guard's handgun from his holster, aimed it down, and blew a hole through his foot. The guard howled in pain as Ashley spun around and fired two shots into the guard's chest. The guard hit the floor hard like he had just been tossed out of a window. Ashley quickly walked over and grabbed the two extra clips from the guard's waist band and shoved them down into her pocket. Her adrenaline was pumping as she moved on throughout the mansion. This was Ashley's first time ever killing a person and to be honest she loved it. She loved how powerful the kill made her feel and she couldn't wait to kill again. A loud noise erupted from behind Ashley. She quickly spun and aimed her gun in the direction of the noise. One of Mr. Clarke's guards limped in her direction looking like he was trying to get out of harm's way. When the guard looked up and spotted the little girl holding the gun he quickly came to a halt. He threw his hands in the air in surrender. "Come on now put the gun down," the guard said in a nerves tone. He looked in the little girl's eyes and saw no fear. "Trust me, you don't want to do this," he said inching his way towards Ashley. He planned on getting as close as he could so he could take the gun from her and beat her to a pulp with it. "Hand me the gun and I promise..." the guard's head exploded like a tomato silencing him forever. Ashley shot him in the head and continued on throughout the mansion as if nothing had ever happened. The mansion was so big that it felt like she was moving in circles. Throughout the mansion it seemed as if she had spotted dozens of dead bodies. All of the dead bodies only told her one thing, and that was that Angela was somewhere inside the mansion.

***

Frank eased up behind an officer and put a bullet in the back of his head dropping the officer where he stood. Frank moved through the mansion like a ghost taking out officers left and right. He positioned himself in a dark area and stood taking police officers out. He took pride in killing the officers. If it was one thing he couldn't stand, it was a snitch and a cop. Frank heard a sharp noise coming from his right. He quickly threw himself onto the floor of the hallway and fired close quarters at the silhouette hulking in the door frame. A grunt came from the shooter before his body crashed face first into the hardwood floor. Frank quickly hopped up to his feet and removed his suit jacket as he continued on throughout the mansion. He knew Angela was somewhere in the mansion. All he had to do was locate her and kill her. There was no way he was going to let her get away with killing his wife. The police had started to over power Mr. Clarke's men as more and more cops showed up and entered the mansion.

Out of nowhere a muscular police officer sprang from around the corner and slapped Frank's gun from his hand. He took a fighting stance and then moved towards the assassin. This was a stupid move. Frank fired off a quick sharp ten punch combo. Now the officer was suffering blow after blow, bending, grunting, bleeding, and going down hard and fast. Ten hard and fast blows from Frank's right hand to his face and ribs left his face broken beyond belief. If the officer was lucky, he'd wake up pissing blood, a tube in his nose, and a shit bag strapped to his hip. Frank picked up the officer's gun and moved on down the hallway where he spotted two more officers. The one with the

A.K. was Frank's first target. He suffered a quick headshot and so did the man standing to his left. Both men toppled face down into the floor, souls evicting from their bodies before they realized what was going on. As Frank moved throughout the mansion, he spotted a figure standing at the end of the hall. A figure dressed in an all black ninja suit stood waiting. From the silhouette, Frank could tell that the body at the end of the hall belonged to a woman.

28

LET'S GET THIS OVER AND DONE WITH

Angela stood at the end of the hall with a silenced .380 in both hands. Her eyes set on her final target coming down the hall towards her. All types of thoughts ran through Angela's mind as she watched Frank walk towards her in what seemed like a slow motion. The closer he got, the more Angela wanted to kill him and get this over with once and for all.

"So finally we meet face to face," Frank said standing a few feet away from Angela. "You know I could of shot you from all the way down the hall right?"

"And what fun would that be?" Angela capped back. She knew that Frank wanted to look in her eyes before he killed her because of what she had done to his wife.

"So how do you want to do this?" Frank asked. "Hand to hand or you want to shoot it out?"

A smirk danced on Angela's lips. "Hand to hand of course," was her answer.

Frank smiled, but deep down inside he knew a hand to hand battle with Angela wouldn't be a walk in the park. She didn't become the number one assassin for nothing. "Well let's get this party started shall we," he said tossing his weapon down to the floor.

"Where's Ashley?" Angela asked as she ripped the black mask from her face and tossed it down to the floor.

"I personally put a bullet in her pretty little head," Frank said letting out a strong laugh that came from the bottom of his gut. That last comment drove Angela over the edge. She tossed her guns down to the floor and took off full speed towards Frank. Angela tackled Frank. She hit him hard and took him off his feet as the two went crashing out the window. The two floated through the air and then grunted as they both hit the ground hard.

Frank made it to his feet first and charged Angela. He came at her hard, threw elbows, and fist hard enough to break a person's nose. Angela blocked as many of the blows as she could while a few of them slipped in between her guard. Angela grabbed both of Frank's arms to stop the blows from raining in as she delivered a sharp knee to the pit of Frank's stomach causing him to double over in pain.

Several police officers gathered around Angela and Frank. Before they could separate the two assassins and arrest them, Detective Washington stepped in. "Let them handle their business and we'll arrest them when it's over!" he shouted. With that being said, the police formed a circle around Angela and Frank and enjoyed the show.

Angela tried to break Frank's nose with a knee to the face, but he blocked the knee and landed a stiff hook to her ribcage. Angela stumbled back a few steps before taking her stance. Since Frank was in attack mode she'd figure it'd be easier if she tried to counter him instead of fighting him head on. Frank threw a stiff jab at Angela's face, but when the punch got there, Angela's face was no longer there. Angela weaved the punch and landed a sharp kick on the lower part of Frank's leg. Frank's eyes looked down at his leg and that was the split second that Angela needed. She lunged through the air and landed a flying elbow in the center of Frank's face turning his face into a bloody mess.

Frank touched his face and his fingers came away bloody. He paused for a second and then in a blind rage, he went after Angela. She didn't back down. Instead she moved towards the fight, not away from the man who was twice her size. She landed a hard blow to the side of Frank's head. He ignored the blow, grabbed Angela and lifted her over his head, then tossed her down to the ground as if she was a piece of trash. Angela crashed hard, landing on unforgiving rocks and concrete. Before Angela got a chance to make it back up to her feet, Frank kicked her in the face as if he were kicking a field goal. He then hopped on top of her and began to pound away at her face. Angela lay on the ground trying to block as many blows as she could, but she got hit with so many punches that she felt like she was getting jumped.

Detective Washington stood on the sideline watching Frank pound Angela out. He felt so bad for Angela and he wanted to jump into the fight and see if Frank would be as successful doing a man the way he was doing a woman. But all he could do at the moment was cheer Angela on. Thoughts of shooting Frank in the head crossed his mind the more he watched the man beat up on Angela. If the fight didn't turn around soon, he would have no choice but to get involved. Angela defended herself the best she could from down on her back. She grabbed a hold of Frank's arm and flipped around on the ground applying an arm bar trying the snap his arm at the elbow.

"Arrrgh!!!" Frank growled as his eyes widened with pain, until finally he heard his bone snap. Once Angela heard Frank's bone snap she quickly hopped to her feet and delivered field goal like kicks to his face.

"Come on motherfucker!" Angela growled. Her face was now a bloody mess and she could only see out of one eye, due to the fact that Frank had swollen her eye shut with all of those punches. Angela yanked her belt from out of the waist of her suit as she watched Frank stumble back to his feet. She wrapped the belt around her right hand and snapped it out. The belt buckle stabbed like a knife striking Frank in the eye like the bite of a cobra. Angela swung the belt with bad intentions as she battered Frank's head, hands, and face.

Having no other options Frank ran and went airborne, taking his knee straight to Angela's wounded face. He hit Angela hard, and then went down even harder. The knee to the face forced Angela to drop the belt down to the ground. With only one arm, Frank would now have to change his attack method and use his legs more. When Angela made it back to her feet, Frank landed a skipping side kick. The kick hit Angela flush on the chin putting her down. Frank patiently waited for Angela to crawl back to her feet and then landed a roundhouse to Angela's face. She partially blocked the kick, but the side of her head took most of the impact. The kick didn't drop Angela, but it left her dazed and somewhat dizzy. Frank quickly followed up with a chop to Angela's throat and then a powerful kick that landed directly in the pit of her stomach.

Angela stood with a stocked look on her face as she held her throat with both hands. The blow to her throat did something to her windpipe that prevented her from being able to take in any air.

Frank smirked when he saw the look of defeat in Angela's eyes. He then charged Angela, grabbed her as he hit her hard, lifting her up, both of them airborne, crashing down where the lake water began. Frank landed two stiff punches to Angela's face and then she felt the rush of the lake water. The water was freezing and the salt was stinging. Angela struggled to get a lung full of air, tried to hold her breath while Frank pushed her head under the water and held it there. Angela's world quickly vanished as she was forced into a liquid darkness. As Angela's head was held under water her life began to flash before her eyes. She saw all the fun times she'd had with James, then her mind drifted to The White Shadow, then drifted to all the training she'd done all throughout her life, then her mind drifted to Mr.

Biggz, then to Ashley, then finally it drifted to the man that had her head held under water. Angela's eyes widened as she could no longer hold her breath any longer. The sound of a gun being fired sounded off loudly then suddenly Frank released his grip.

Angela's head sprang from out the water like a jack in the box as she quickly sucked in as much air as she could. She looked up and saw Frank staring at her with a hole in the center of his head. He toppled down on top of Angela in slow motion. Behind Frank stood Ashley holding a smoking gun in her hands.

Ashley dropped the gun and ran to Angela's aid and helped pull her out of the water.

"I knew you would come for me," Ashley said with a big smile on her face. Not knowing what to say back, all she could do was cry. Her mind and body had both been through a lot, and at that very moment she was so happy to see little Ashley.

"I saved your life," Ashley kept repeating over and over. "I saved The Teflon Queen's life," she said proudly.

"Thank you," Angela cried as she hugged Ashley tightly. She knew she was soaking wet, but she didn't care. At the moment she wanted Ashley to know that she loved her and would always treat her like a daughter. "Thank you so much!"

"I was there for you," Ashley said as tears began to escape her eyes. "I was there for you! I told you I could do it! I told you!" she kept saying. Just as Angela was about to tell Ashley how proud of her she was, two F.B.I. agents roughly slammed her over on her stomach and cuffed her hands behind her back.

"Noooo!" Ashley yelled as she went to attack one of the agents, but Detective Washington quickly restrained her.

"Calm down," Detective Washington whispered in Ashley's ear as the both of them had to watch Angela being shoved in the back of an unmarked car. In the car next to Angela sat Mr. Clarke. He too was in handcuffs.

Angela sat in the back of the agent's car and knew that this would be the last minutes of her being a free woman. She had been on so many wanted lists that she knew they would more than likely put her under the jail. Of course she could have easily picked her cuffs, but at the moment Angela was simply tired of all the ripping and running. That part of her life was now officially over. She mouthed the word, *"I love you"* to Ashley as the agents drove her away.

"I love you too!" Ashley cried as she watched the Feds take Angela away.

"Everything is going to be alright," Detective Washington said as he rubbed Ashley's back.

"I'm never going to see her again am I?" Ashley asked in between sobs.

"I don't know," Detective Washington mumbled as a tear escaped his eye. He felt bad for Angela and Ashley. After getting to know Angela he realized she wasn't a bad person, but just a woman who had made some bad decisions in her life. He felt even worse for Ashley. With both of her parents dead she was destined for a life in the system and he knew the system was no place for a little innocent girl like Ashley to grow up.

"What's going to happen to me now?" Ashley asked looking up at Detective Washington with tears in her eyes.

Detective Washington looked down at the floor and said. "I don't know."

"I'm going to a foster home aren't I?" Ashley asked in a knowing tone. She may not have known much, but that she did know.

"I'm not sure," Detective Washington lied. He didn't have to heart to tell her the truth. The entire scene was breaking his heart.

"Is there any way that you can get Angela out of jail? She really is a good person," Ashley said.

"I'll see what I can do," Detective Washington said. He knew there was nothing that he could do to help Angela. Too much had already been done and nothing could be taken back or over looked.

"So I guess this is it then huh?" Ashley said wiping her eyes dry.

Detective Washington nodded his head and then mumbled, "Yes."

29

THREE MONTHS LATER

Detective Washington sat in front of a steel table in an empty room at a super maximum security woman's jail out in the middle of nowhere. He'd been trying to get up to the jail and visit Angela for the past three months and finally they allowed for him to do so. Detective Washington sat for thirty minutes before several guards finally escorted Angela into the room. She sported an orange jumper and on her feet were a pair if cheap slippers. Chains hung from her wrist, ankles, and waist. One would have thought that she was some kind cruel monster. The officers helped Angela down into her seat and then stood directly behind her.

"That won't be necessary," Detective Washington told the officers.

"You got ten minutes!" the red faced officer barked then left the room leaving Angela and Detective Washington alone in the room.

"How have you been holding up in here?" Detective Washington asked.

Angela chuckled. "How do you think I'm doing? The judge gave me triple life."

Angela wore her hair pulled back into a ponytail and one long thick braid hung down her back.

"That's better than the needle."

"Speak for yourself."

"I'm going to do the best I can to make sure that you have everything you need while you're in here," Detective Washington told her.

"Why are you helping me?" Angela asked.

"Because sometimes even the strongest people need a little help," Detective Washington replied.

"I appreciate it," Angela said as tears began to stream down her face. "How's Ashley been holding up?"

Detective Washington broke eye contact before he answered. "She ran away from her foster home two months ago and no one has seen or heard from her since."

Those words cut through Angela like a knife. After getting to know Ashley she knew how much of a good kid she was.

Detective Washington slipped Angela a picture. "I know she would of wanted you to have this."

Angela looked down and saw the picture that she and Ashley had taken right before Mr. Clarke's men had bum rushed the house. "Thank you."

"Don't mention it," Detective Washington said. "The last time Ashley's foster parents saw her they said that Ashley had told them not to call her Ashley anymore, but instead to call her The Teflon Princess."

"I have a safe house that has close to five hundred thousand dollars in it. Write down the address," Angela said giving Detective Washington the address. "I need you to send me money every month and you can use the rest of the money on whatever you need for yourself. I won't have much use for it in here anyway."

"No that's your money," he said quickly. "I'll send you some of it every month like you said."

"You can use the money, but just promise me one thing," Angela said looking Detective Washington in the eye.

"Anything."

"Promise me that you'll find Ashley and look after her. Use some of that money to give her a better life," Angela said. "Show her the right way to live."

"I promise! I got you," Detective Washington said as he stood up and kissed Angela on the lips just as the officers ran up in the room and escorted Angela back to her cell.

Detective Washington stood there and watched how roughly the officers handled Angela. Deep down inside he wished that he could have helped Angela escape from the mansion somehow before she got arrested. Right now he was the only person that Angela had in her corner and he promised not to let her down. The first thing tomorrow morning he planned on hitting the pavement and searching for Ashley. He knew he had to find her before something bad happened to her.

TO BE CONTINUED.....

Email the author silkwhite212@yahoo.com

Books by Good2Go Authors on Our Bookshelf

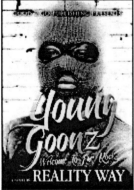

Good2Go Films Presents

To order books, please fill out the order form below:
To order films please go to www.good2gofilms.com

Name: _____

Address: _____

City: _____ State: _____ Zip Code: _____

Phone: _____

Email: _____

Method of Payment: ☐ Check ☐ VISA ☐ MASTERCARD

Credit Card#: _____

Name as it appears on card: _____

Signature: _____

Item Name	Price	Qty	Amount
He Loves Me. He Loves You Not - Mychea	$14.99		
He Loves Me. He Loves You Not 2 - Mychea	$14.99		
Married To Da Streets – Silk White	$14.99		
My Boyfriend's Wife - Mychea	$14.99		
Never Be The Same – Silk White	$14.99		
Stranded – Silk White	$14.99		
Slumped – Jason Brent	$14.99		
Tears of a Hustler - Silk White	$14.99		
Tears of a Hustler 2 - Silk White	$14.99		
Tears of a Hustler 3 - Silk White	$14.99		
Tears of a Hustler 4- Silk White	$14.99		
Tears of a Hustler 5 – Silk White	$14.99		
The Teflon Queen – Silk White	$14.99		
The Teflon Queen 2 – Silk White	$14.99		
The Teflon Queen – 3 – Silk White	$14.99		
Young Goonz – Reality Way	$14.99		
Subtotal:			
Tax:			
Shipping (Free) U.S. Media Mail:			
Total:			

Make Checks Payable To:
Good2Go Publishing
7311 W Glass Lane
Laveen. AZ 85339

CPSIA information can be obtained at www.ICGtesting.com
Printed in the USA
LVOW07s1705090116

469908LV00017B/906/P